WHAT'S PEARL GOT TO DO WITH IT

TO DO WITH IT

Sun Over Star Gazer Island, Book Two

DEBRA
CLOPTON

What's Pearl Got To Do With It
Copyright © 2025 Debra Clopton Parks

What's Pearl Got To Do With It

"Don't be afraid to love… Let your heart free."
Nearly four years after losing her friend, Olivia's words still echo in Pearl's heart.

Photographer Pearl McConnell has spent her life traveling the world, capturing breathtaking places and writing stories that stir souls. But somewhere between takeoffs and deadlines, a quiet ache has taken root. She has everything she ever wanted… so why does it feel like something's missing?

Her sister Dora has just married and is taking flight with her new husband. Kat is back and forth between her seaside restaurants in Texas and the Hawaiian islands. But Pearl—grateful for the life she leads—suddenly finds herself craving stillness, family, and a chance to catch her breath.

Returning home to Star Gazer Island, Pearl hopes that time with loved ones will quiet the restlessness in her spirit. But when she's offered a lucrative assignment to profile Brant Randall, a reclusive bull-riding legend turned horse trainer now living at the McIntyre Ranch, everything shifts.

Brant has no interest in anymore fame or fanfare. He's here to start fresh, far from headlines and expectations. Pearl's presence is a disruption—but her eyes see more than just the man the world remembers. And when their paths cross under a moonlit Texas sky, something stirs in both of them… something unexpected, undeniable, and impossible to ignore.

She's trying to slow down. He's trying to disappear. But life—and love—on Star Gazer Island has a way of showing up right when you need it most.

Life on Star Gazer Island is about to stir the tides again, as Pearl discovers that sometimes the clearest picture of love is the one you never meant to take… and that coming home might just be the story worth capturing after all.

CHAPTER ONE

Pearl McConnell smoothed the waist of her teal-toned silk dress, shifted her shoulders back, and inhaled through her nose, making herself do so to calm the tension radiating through her—as always before entering a large gathering of people. Even if it was a gathering of friends and family she loved with everything in her heart, tension still tried to overcome her.

So odd, since she was known for her calm, embracing spirit and creative mind—which she fought hard to make sure everyone still believed she had. Even her family had no idea of the pressure she sometimes felt before large gatherings, such as the photography shows she attended while traveling for her photo shoots.

Shoots she loved and felt called to do—but still, there was the appearance she had to keep up.

Even when this odd feeling of unease surrounded her, she always, like now, shoved the unease aside and walked through the tall, wide opening of the giant white tent and into the prestigious Texas cattlemen's gathering. The McIntyres and several other huge cattle ranches held this a few times a year here in South Texas. She took in the glamorous setup of round tables, white tablecloths, glistening glasses, elegant decorations, and people filling the room. Dressed-up people stood around talking, laughing, and enjoying the moments before the steak dinner—and then the auction, starting with the famous jeweled ornament.

This was the largest private cattle auction of the year.

Her dad, along with several other major cattle ranchers from the area—from Star Gazer Island all the way to the Hill Country and even past that—ranches like the McCoys, the Monahans, and the Valentines—would participate. Everyone in the cattle industry was here, and as always, they were excited for the big night.

She was too. Though she traveled the world taking pictures and writing for big magazines, she was glad to be here for this premier event—hanging out with her family that she loved with all her heart.

So why was she feeling this unease?

She adored this group of people. Her gaze crossed the crowded room and found her brother Matt, his arm around his wife, so happy since marrying Kelley after the hardship of losing his first wife, Olivia, almost four years ago. Pearl knew Olivia was happy looking down from above at the glow on Matt's face—an expression that told of the joy in his heart.

Her gaze then shifted to her sister Dora and Dora's new husband, Hawk. They were deeply engaged in conversation with Kelley and Matt. Pearl loved that quiet Dora had found an incredible man who had brought her out of her little cubbyhole of aloneness she'd surrounded herself with since losing Olivia. Seeing the twinkle in her sister's eyes and the beaming smile on her face sent peace through Pearl.

Life was good. Dora was about to start flying all over the United States with Hawk, the remodeling-home-builder-extraordinaire. Dora's employees at her wonderful store in Stargaze would run the store while she traveled. Finally, her little sister was going to enjoy herself and her new life—not pinned down to her small seashell beach and her broken heart.

Looking at them, Pearl knew she was blessed. Her fingers itched for her camera—this picture said everything about how love worked. This is what she did:

captured moments that told stories.

That ability gave her a business that didn't require her to be pinned down anywhere. She traveled all over the world with her photography, making sure her photos stood out. She had a sharp eye and knew it—there was no denying it because her work put her in the spotlight.

But tonight, she was home in the town she loved. In the state she loved. After all, Texas was the size of several countries she'd just traveled over to get back.

As much as she traveled, she loved Star Gazer Island the most—and she was here for some time off.

Though she hadn't said it to her sisters, she had a feeling Kat was suspicious. At their parents' house the other night, Kat had asked where she'd be off to next, and Pearl had simply replied, "I'm sticking around here for a little while."

Thankfully, Kat hadn't pressed her. She'd just hitched a brow. "Well, I'm not. I'm heading back to Kona and the other islands."

"Like that surprises me." Pearl had laughed, and her sister had too.

Kat was always on the move and had just come home for this big show that they all loved attending together. Then she was off again to one of her restaurants.

Standing there now, taking everything in as her

thoughts rolled, Pearl heard her name called. She saw Kat weaving her way through the round tables toward her. Pearl watched her—so did many of the cowboys she was passing. But Kat's attention was only on Pearl.

She'd seen men look at Kat before, and at her too. Pearl always kept a calculated expression on her face— the one she used in crowds. Not harsh, not stuck-up— just pleasant. She'd worked on that look, just like she worked on her photos.

For her, it wasn't about being embraced—it was about being approachable in business settings. And it came in handy, especially now. She was used to men staring at her, making conversation, and asking her out. Sometimes she went. Most times she didn't. She wasn't a loner, but she didn't date long—never attached to one place.

She didn't know how Kat reacted to the stares when she was alone in crowds, but right now her attention was on Pearl—and every cowboy in the room knew it.

"Pearl, you look gorgeous," Kat gushed, wrapping her in a tight hug.

"Right back at you." Pearl laughed, noting how Kat's wavy auburn hair swirled around her shoulders. Her sister's golden eyes sparkled like lightning on a dark night.

They loved each other fiercely—but were

opposites. Pearl, with her pearl-toned hair and soft, cream evening dress, liked dressing up. There was nothing wrong with it. And as always, she had on her high-heeled, almost-not-there sandals that she loved to wear to parties.

Normally, her outfit was cargo pants, hiking shoes—clothes that could handle the terrain wherever her photography took her. Heels and dresses weren't work attire.

"You look beautiful, Kat. As always," she said.

"Thank you. I'm glad you stayed."

"I'm glad to be here," Pearl said, her eyes drifting back to her family. "Glad to watch those two couples—our married brother and our married sister—chatting away happily. I'm still thrilled for quiet Dora as she and Hawk head off to the San Juan Islands… her, instead of me."

"I love it," Kat said. "A lot. The timing of those two meeting was perfect."

"Yes, it was," Pearl agreed. "And now she'll be helping him renovate homes all over the place. He brought her out of her shell. Now our quiet, loner sister might out-fly us."

Kat laughed. "I know. She loves remodeling. Who knew?"

"Life is full of surprises." Pearl sighed. "Look at

her—she's just beaming."

Kat's shoulder bumped Pearl's as they stood watching Dora. Matt caught Pearl's eye and grinned, waving them over.

"Our brother sees what we see," Kat said. "We all owe handsome Hawk for that new spark in Dora."

"Yes, we do." Pearl glanced at her sister as Kat raised an eyebrow.

"So, sister, I don't know if you realize it, but there are cowboys all around us who have eyes on you," Kat said.

"They have eyes on you too, and you're as not interested as I am. I mean, honestly, I'm just not ready." She almost groaned the words.

Kat sighed. "Me either. But look how happy our brother and sister are."

"They radiate," Pearl said.

She looked around the massive, beautifully decorated tent. She spotted so many familiar faces—but then, her gaze locked onto a tall cowboy she didn't know. He wore a starched white shirt beneath a black western jacket, starched jeans, black boots, and a cowboy hat pulled low over striking, light blue eyes— eyes that were locked on her.

Caught completely off guard by her reaction, she almost gasped—but thankfully didn't.

She hadn't moved at all—just stood frozen, taking in his strong jawline and the subtle curve of his lips as they hitched slightly, stealing even more of her breath.

Then he tipped his hat, turned and walked away, disappearing into the crowd, leaving her standing there stunned.

Her heart thundered, her breath caught, and she felt something she'd never felt before. It was like seeing the perfect photo shot—breathtaking and alive, not just because it could make her money, but because it would move someone's soul.

It moved hers, in that moment.

"Your brain has gone somewhere," Kat said, nudging her.

"Sorry. I got distracted."

Kat scanned the room, clearly trying to follow Pearl's gaze. Thank goodness the cowboy was gone.

"We best head over to the family," Kat said. "They're auctioning off that gorgeous ornament tonight. Hawk says no one will outbid him."

Pearl focused on the here and now—not the cowboy who had shaken her.

Focus. She did that, her mind shifting to the very talented ornament maker from Mule Hollow who was here. For several years now, the McIntyres had auctioned off one of her jeweled ornaments for a huge price to benefit a special cause. People came just for that.

Tonight, nobody was going to outbid Hawk. He was on a mission. He wanted the ornament for Dora—to hang in their new house, with its glass ceilings and windows designed by their sister-in-law, Kelley. It wouldn't be cheap—but it would be meaningful.

Kat paused. "You know, sometimes we get used to having so much. Hawk's going to win because he can. His hard work and talent make him able, just like us—and the ranchers here. Oil helps. But this?" She gestured around. "This is rare for most people and we've grown used to it."

"Yes," Pearl said. "We have."

Kat's golden eyes held hers. "You and I travel, live our dreams, and we do it with Olivia in our hearts—smiling at us."

Pearl's heart clenched tight. "Yes, we are blessed."

That feeling was one reason she was taking time off. Olivia's sweet smile filled her mind, and she needed to escape the emotions that came with it. She brought her focus back to their conversation.

"But I don't live fancy," she added. "We don't flaunt it. These folks don't either. They're just... I don't know. Hardworking. Blessed."

"Yes," Kat said. "But I know you. Sometimes you

wonder what life would be like if you hadn't been born into this."

Pearl sighed. "True. But I'm not taking it for granted."

Kat stepped back and crossed her arms. "So what's going on? Our brother, our sister—we've all had big life changes. Is there something you need to talk about?"

Pearl just shook her head. "No. I'm just... I'm going to stay home a while. I'm not taking a job anytime soon. I just feel like sticking around."

Kat blinked. "Wow. That's huge for you. I go back and forth between Texas and Hawaii. You travel the globe."

Pearl laughed. "I do. But I think I'm going to stay put. For now."

"Are you having problems?"

Pearl didn't know what to say. "No, I'm fine. I just want to be home for a while."

Kat didn't quite believe her, but she let it go. "All right, then. Let's talk to our people. Greet, meet, and eat."

Pearl gave a small laugh and followed her dynamic sister into the crowd. It was celebration night—no matter what confusing thoughts swirled in her mind. She was here. With her family. Exactly where she wanted—*needed*—to be.

CHAPTER TWO

Brant Randall was stunned by the beautiful, breathtaking lady who had walked in the door. He could tell by the look in her gaze when she came in that she was used to being stared at. Probably hit on a lot, but she was calm, collected, and elegant.

She had hair, the color of a, he let his brain work for a minute… a pearl. His grandmother had owned a set of exquisite pearls that she'd left to him before she'd passed away of a heart attack. He'd been five but in her will she'd left them to him. She'd remembered special moments when she'd held him in her lap and he would play with them, sometimes twist them. Once, he'd twisted harder than he'd meant to and the string broke. Pearls had erupted across the room like tiny bowling balls looking for escape. But his sweet grandmother hadn't complained, she got down on the floor with him and they'd gathered them all up one by one.

He must have had a horrified look on his face, because he knew the necklace had belonged to her mother, given to her by his great-grandfather and was all she had left of them. But she'd looked at him, while still on her knees and said, "Don't worry, sweet boy, all things in life have their limits and when they break you just repair them."

So true, not just physically but emotionally he'd learned and even now he was trying to do exactly that.

His grandmother had also pointed out that she loved pearls. "Because each one had its own unique tone. It wasn't white, it wasn't beige, it was just a soft tone that sparkled in its own way." His grandmother had a great way about her and now, from where he was standing near the side exit of the tent. he looked across the room at the eye-catching lady. The lady who was really bringing back a wonderful rush of memories of his grandmother and her pearls.

He wondered what her name was… she was unique—his mind instantly jerked back to the here and now when her gaze shifted from the other attractive lady beside her and locked with his. Even from a distance her eyes had a unique blueness to them. He had blue eyes too, but they were different, light while hers were deeper with a touch of sunshine radiating from them. Suddenly her eyes connected to his and she must have realized he was staring at her. She met his gaze straight on, didn't look away, just stared back.

He hitched another smile, just a half smile, an acknowledgement smile. Not that he was looking for attraction right now but who could *not* smile at something striking like her? It was like looking at a piece of art or a picturesque, pleasing photograph. Then, getting his brain back, he reminded himself that he was here at this ranch to focus on moving forward with a new career. And he was here because he was friends with the McIntyre brothers, Jackson and Dallas, who he knew because he too had been a champion bull rider but had given it up in order to have a new life.

Brant was here to do the same, at least that was what was on his mind. He was here for at least a couple of months because of a back injury that he was recovering from, and training horses, which was something he loved to do when not bull riding.

He had a decision to make. Dallas had been smart and gotten out of bull riding before it was too late to keep himself in shape. Before he got too injured to live life comfortably. This was something he was struggling with right now while he took time off here on the

McIntyre's family ranch.

He was a champion too, knew how to win and had sponsors he was responsible for who paid him to do what he did out in the rodeo arena. And there was plenty of pressure to keep doing what he was doing…

They didn't know he had a lower back problem. He hid it, held his hips in and his shoulders back and walked straight. Sometimes it took gritting his teeth when it hurt too bad, like now, but he always made it.

But would he always make a comeback? That was what was on his mind, *not* the gorgeous pearl-looking lady who had taken his mind off of the pain in his back for the moment. Twice, since he was locked on her again. She looked away and he focused on the room full of people once more. People who had fancied up just to bid on some cattle and some horses.

And that was one of his specialties. He knew a good horse when he saw it. Saw what it could be, not what it was at the moment, untrained.

He saw Jackson McIntyre waving him over toward where he and his brother were talking. Brant was living on the McIntyre's huge ranch in one of their cabins, where it was set up for him to start breaking and training horses for them and anyone else interested.

He reached Jackson. "Y'all definitely know how to throw a party and call it business."

Jackson grinned. "It's all business, just like having some fun with friends while doing it."

"And sell some livestock and horses too," Dallas added, grinning.

The man was his age, strong and able, but retired from bull riding and looked healthy. Brant gave him a nod and a smile. "I've heard they come from all over Texas."

Jackson nodded. "Thankfully in our area we have some master ranchers with outstanding livestock and horses that others want. And we're glad to have you join the group."

"I'm glad to be here. Dallas warned me there were a lot of people coming tonight and he wasn't kidding."

"I don't lie," Dallas drawled out as his gaze swept the room.

Jackson looked at Brant. "Don't go off and hole up somewhere because there are a lot of people who'll be looking for you. I've been telling them all how good you are with your calm way of taming and training horses. I've got to get this show going so I'll talk to you later."

"Thanks," Brant said to Jackson as the cowboy headed toward the front stage. He was glad he was here. He was a famous bull rider, so it shocked people when they realized how good he was at calmly breaking and training horses of all types. When riding a furious bucking bull for more than half his life it was a relief to help a horse learn how to be useful on a ranch.

Better yet when one he'd trained competed and won a competition, it gave Brant a satisfaction that even winning a bull riding event didn't give him.

The difference of being on the back of a raging bull, where he'd learned he could ride and let go of the anger that had raged through him growing up. But now, it was the peace that came to him while he was calmly helping a wild or angry horse learn what he'd learned, to adjust and take things in a better way… made life easier. Better.

For him and the horse. And now he was planning to make a living at doing just that. Though his sponsors had other ideas. They wanted him out in the arena, winning and selling their products. Plus, he had an interview coming up that he was having to adjust to. He had to do it, had agreed to do so for all of his sponsors. A major deal he wasn't looking forward to doing. He hadn't told any of his sponsors he wasn't going back into the arena on the back of a bull. But he would.

It was time; his lower back throbbed as usual, reminding him that he was making the right decision.

"I agree with my brother," Dallas said.

Brant pulled his hurting hip in. "I promise you, they'll be tamed with soft words and calm training."

"I've seen some outstanding trainers, and you're one of them," Dallas continued. "Word is getting out and I know they're coming to do that write-up on you about your bull riding, but also because word has gotten out about the way you tame a horse."

The interview. That wasn't what he wanted to think about tonight but he nodded at his friend's words. "I'm glad to be here."

And he was. This was going to be a new adventure—the interview, he'd think positively about since it might give him the spotlight to focus on moving forward with the training. Might help his sponsors see another avenue for them too.

Jackson stepping onto the main platform drew their attention. But, then Brant's gaze roamed the tent—and whether he wanted it to or not—it landed on the pearl blonde-haired woman standing in the distance talking with some cowboys, an older man, and some pretty women, one of the ladies she'd been talking to earlier. They all looked like they were having a wonderful time and the blonde was smiling radiantly.

His pulse increased even from this distance, he pulled his gaze away and focused on the stage. He was not ready to try and find a new start here in the direction of romance, but there was no denying that something about that woman drew him like twilight over the blue ocean.

And despite fighting it, he knew he was going to at least have to find out her name.

* * *

Before the buying of the cattle started, Jackson McIntyre stepped up to the microphone. "Welcome. So, we're going to start this night off with the annual ornament auction. We buy the specially made ornament and then we auction it off for even more. The money goes to your donation choice, so that makes the higher price benefit others and enables the extraordinarily talented lady standing there—Naomi—to continue doing what she does. It gives her joy and makes all of you happy being able to hang these jewels up in high places and watch them dance in the sunlight. Real jeweled ornaments like this one bring these high prices, but her real joy is creating Christmas ornaments that anyone can afford and can be found online or at her Christmas tree farm in Mule Hollow."

"Now we're going to start the auction for this beauty, named 'A World of Love,' and the winner of the auction will be able to donate the money the bidding brings in to whatever cause they want to donate to."

Everyone's gaze—well, everyone that Pearl could see—came around and landed on Pearl's brother and then his sweet wife, Kelley, who had lost her dad when a building had caved in, and he had rescued her by throwing her out from underneath it. The house that they had been building was to help people. She was an incredible builder and hadn't been able to build for a long time after that but now she was kept busy building stunning glass buildings or homes with glass ceilings to give people the feeling of being outside. And she also gave back to her dad's legacy, building smaller homes for people in need. And tonight, Dora's husband planned on winning the bid so Dora would have the jeweled ornament for their home. And the money would be donated to Kelley's foundation.

Pearl felt good inside as the bidding started high and quickly went higher as Hawk and wealthy ranchers from all across Texas competed for the great cause they knew it would go toward if they won. But mostly they all had fun making Hawk sweat a little before they all backed off and let him win.

Pearl gave him and smiling Dora a hug. "It's going to look perfect in that outstanding remodeled home of yours."

"I think so too," Dora said. "But it's also going to be my reminder of what Olivia wanted for all of us. Happiness is what will fill me when it sends sparkles across the living room. But also, knowing the money helps Kelley's building group give back."

Kelley was standing there smiling and Pearl hugged her too. Her heart felt light seeing the happiness in both Kelley's and Dora's expressions. And in Hawk's and her brother Matt's eyes too, knowing their wives were happy.

Emotion filled Pearl, tugged hard at her heart knowing from heaven Olivia had to be happy too, seeing their joy and love.

Pearl's heart throbbing, she pulled her small camera from her dress pocket. She had huge cameras, but this was family and times she didn't want to miss, so her tiny one worked.

After a while, they all took their seats at their tables and had a fantastic meal, but then, feeling restless, Pearl eased out of the tent at the side exit and into the moonlight and the stillness of the night. She always needed quiet time and space after being in a crowded room, even those filled like tonight with friends and family.

She breathed in the fresh air, looked up at the sky as emotion filled her. She used to escape the crowded tent and come out here with Olivia—that was before she got sick and before she married Matt.

The thought had Pearl's eyes tear up and she brushed them away. Olivia, her sweet friend, had told her not to mourn. And it had been four years, but tonight, seeing Matt so happy with Kelley and Dora with Hawk, they'd all moved forward like Olivia had wanted.

Standing there looking into the darkness she knew she'd done good, living life with happiness like Olivia wanted her to do. She loved knowing she'd made Olivia's wish for her come true. But lately something more was missing and she knew it. And that feeling had brought her home.

What was going on in her life had nothing really to do with losing Olivia. No, it was just tonight this—the way she often was among people, but was also alone.

She traveled the world on her own and lately she'd started wondering what it would feel like to share a night like tonight with someone.

CHAPTER THREE

Brant had been standing outside looking up at the moon. He was leaning against the end of the fence line that was several feet away from the tent's side exit. It was a bright shimmering moon tonight, giving him something nice to look at as he leaned against the railing, second rail from the top so his hip had relief from the strain it was feeling.

He'd been startled when the woman he'd been admiring, who he'd seen taking pictures of the winner of the ornament, and he'd instantly known who he was seeing.

Once they'd introduced the winners, he realized that this was the McConnell family. And the lovely lady with the camera and the pearly hair was Pearl

McConnell. The renowned photographer and article writer who traveled the world taking photographs. He should have already figured it out with all the thinking about pearls she'd caused in his brain.

The other one with the auburn curled hair was the third sister, and from the conversation he could hear from the cowboys a few steps away from him, both of them traveled all the time. The cowboys said they were hard to keep up with. And he almost laughed out loud when they started talking about if they ever did settle down here in town, who could win their hearts?

He'd walked out of the tent then instead of laughing and telling the three cowboys they probably didn't stand a chance with either of the world travelers. This was one moment he could thank his hip for keeping him out of trouble.

So here he was leaning against the fence railing like he was casually watching the moonlight out here alone. And then she had appeared. If she'd turned, she would have seen him, but instead she'd turned slightly away looking to the left, not the right where he was.

This was going to be awkward and he started to speak quietly, as if talking to one of his wild horses so he wouldn't startle her, but in that moment she turned and froze.

"You."

"Sorry, I was about to tell you I was here. I didn't mean to startle you. I'm Brant Randall, friend of the McIntyre's."

She relaxed, thankfully. "Nice to meet you, I'm Pearl McConnell. It's an wonderful night, isn't it?"

He smiled, relieved she wasn't going to run. "Yes, it is. That's one thing I've been impressed with since I've been here these last three weeks is how beautiful it is out here. So that was your brother-in-law who won the ornament. He wasn't going to lose."

A brilliant smile spread across her face and the moonlight caught it and her glowing eyes. Goodness. Pearl McConnell had a smile to die for.

"Yes, so now the McConnells have two keepsakes in the family. When Dora saw the one Matt won at an auction, she loved it so much that Hawk wanted her to have one too." She stopped talking as if her mind went somewhere private and he almost asked her to keep talking.

But he kept his mouth closed. He'd straightened up but now relaxed against the iron fence and to his surprise she stepped forward and did the same, not looking in any hurry to get away.

He liked that. The last thing he wanted to do was scare somebody in the darkness. He knew he had a toughness about him that she obviously wasn't worried about. Then it struck him that maybe she needed to be.

"Do you always relax out in the dark with men?"

She looked at him like he was crazy. "Of course, I don't. You have got to be kidding me. If there was anything about you to give me worries about my safety I'd be on alert. I'm well-trained. And…" She paused, a not-happy look crossing her expression. "Well, part of being well-trained is that you don't walk out in the dark. But, though I did relax a little too much, believe me, if needed, I would have taken care of myself."

"I don't know about that," he said, speaking maybe more than he should. "I was standing over here when you first came out looking all sad and worried. You had no idea I was over here."

She bit her lip, looked thoughtful. "Okay, you're right. I was distracted and I wasn't paying attention, but I'm home. I mean, here, I can relax. When I'm traveling the world by myself, no, I don't. I am in constant watch."

Hearing the hesitation but certainty in her words, he got it. With the way his hip was hurting he'd come outside so no one might see it in his expression. His hip was better since he hadn't been letting himself be bucked around on the back of an angry bull for a few weeks. That helped and his back was going to recover. He changed the subject. "You're the world traveling photographer. And you're home. Are you home for a while? Or are you having another shoot—a photography shoot? Or adventure."

In the dimness her gaze met his and instantly his insides did a back flip. And even in the dim light those blue eyes of hers cut through him like they had inside the building.

"I'm staying home for a little while. I decided I needed a break from traveling. It doesn't mean I won't roam around taking photos. This area is spectacular in the different landscapes, from beaches to rivers, flatland and cattle country. It's just a good area."

He liked it… her words.

"What about you?" she asked.

He hesitated. "I'm taking a break from my bull riding. But I'm out at the McIntyre Ranch breaking horses. They built me an arena out by one of the cabins so that I have my own area. People from all over are bringing me horses."

Her expression was a little confused. "Really? You're a champion bull rider now breaking horses?"

"Yeah, I am, but sometimes you have to—" He cut his sentence off. He'd almost told her he wasn't going to ride a bull anymore.

She cocked her head to the side. "Are you about to say something that you hadn't planned on saying?

26

Believe me, I watch people. I watch the landscape and that includes people's expressions."

He grinned. She had a way. "I watch people, too. That's why I knew you had something on your mind that you haven't said either."

They stared at each other. His heart was suddenly stampeding. "Okay, I'll come clean with you. I'm going to retire. But I'm not telling anyone that just yet and would appreciate it if you didn't mention it either. I'm not real sure why I told you, but if I tell you, it means I obviously trust you for some crazy reason."

Her lips lifted. "Not sure why you trust me, but I won't spread it around."

"Thanks. Now that you know that about me, what's got you out here alone?"

"I'm staying home for a little while, which for me is unusual. I love traveling, seeing the world, creating photos, and working on documentaries on certain things. I enjoy hiking around a new country, getting photo shots that others might love too. So, I'm a little floored by my decision. But when I was in Italy, a little longer in one spot than normal, I liked it. I even thought about making that my home place. But the moment I arrived back on Texas ground, I knew my thought to settle elsewhere was a false alarm, my home is here. But, I'm still unsettled. I love this place. That still has me wondering why I started thinking about settling somewhere else."

He watched how her gaze flickered in the dim light before she focused on the dark pastures beyond him. He was very attracted to the attractive lady.

He placed his elbows back on the fence, relieving the strain on his lower right hip. Then turned his head so he could see her. "So, no one in your family knows you're wondering what you're going to do next?"

"No, they don't, and I'm not going to tell them. I'm just here for a little time off and they're all in for that. Although Kat sees most everything and is a little suspicious, but giving me space. She's very smart and she knows when to give people room. She's the one who told us to back off from my brother when he ran away after losing Olivia. She also knew how to, at least, get Dora to move forward after Olivia's death. But me doing this, and I really can't believe I'm telling you this, but we all loved her very much and made promises to her, I think. I know Dora did and I did too."

He was touched deeply by the love he heard in her voice and saw in the moonlight. "I think that's wonderful to love someone like that." He'd had his grandmother until he was five and cherished every memory of her before she passed away. Had parents until he was six and they still lived in his heart.

"Yes, we were blessed, still are. No one in life knows what is in the next second before them. Or what the future holds. I could pass out right now, dead—I know it's not a very good moment to be saying that but no one usually knows, so we need to be prepared. Olivia knew and her main goal was to enjoy every possible moment she had left and to make sure that each of us would see her in heaven when our time was up."

The words were soft yet powerful. Olivia had definitely had a plan. "She must have been an amazing lady."

"She was. She was our sister long before my brother realized he loved her and wanted her as his wife." She smiled gently and Brant's pulse went unsteady. "She taught us to look at life with excitement and joy in every moment and take no moment for granted. And I don't. But she has me thinking now. It's been four years and I'm here because I'm not sure what I want to celebrate. So, I've come home to Star Gazer Island and the surrounding area for some time with family. That's what Olivia loved, but I feel like I'm missing something."

Brant was totally stunned by her words. The woman seemed to have it all with her career and love her life, like most people thought he did. But this was a connection he hadn't expected, didn't want. He and

Pearl were both searching for the next phase of their lives.

And, now standing straight in the moonlight he had the most powerful feeling that he and Pearl's lives were about to tangle up tightly.

And though he was looking for the next step in his life, the temptation of falling in love wasn't on his list.

* * *

Pearl was not sure why she'd just opened up to this cowboy. But the expression on his face as he listened to her, and the way she felt drawn to him, had all rolled together in that moment.

Maybe it was a God thing. He promised he wouldn't tell anyone what she'd said and he'd opened up to her a little too.

They seemed to be in the same time and moment in their lives in the decisions they would make. What were their next steps? Hers had a little more to it with Olivia being there, but she sensed in his words that there was a little something more in his story too. She had noticed he wasn't standing straight but leaning on that second rail. And she noticed when he straightened up, there had been a slight difference in his expression, just for a second. As if standing straight was a problem. Of course, he was a cowboy, a bull rider and he was breaking horses. None of that was an easy job. Horses didn't like being broken and doing what a cowboy wanted them to do.

She knew there were other ways to break horses that weren't being rough with them. She'd grown up on their huge ranch after all. She'd worked cattle and trained already tamed horses since her dad wouldn't have any of his daughters put in danger's way, as he called it. Kat had gotten on rougher horses in her younger days, before she'd fallen in love with cooking. And Dora too, but she had not pushed her limits. Her mind had always been in the creative mode. That meant that she had paid attention to the ranch and had some stunning photos of working ranches.

"So, do you do the calm, you know, soft spoken, calm way of getting a horse to do what you want... None of the whipping them and kicking them with your spurs, like an old West cowboy?"

He grinned at her words and straightened up, putting his elbow on the fence. "Actually, I do. I ride a bucking horse very seldom. By the time I put my boot in the stirrup, they're almost ready to calmly let me sit on their back. It's a slow, easy, nice way to change the horse's attitude. I respect him or her and they respect me." His words were soft and gentle as he spoke them, sending a calming effect over Pearl.

This man could calm down anyone, she had a feeling, but as he spoke and their gazes locked, her heart trembled and her blood pressure spiked! There was no denying the attraction she felt toward this man. She was attracted to everything about him.

His looks, his build, his calmness, his serenity. In that moment, she wanted to take a photo of the man, the way he looked standing there in the moonlight, his gaze locked with hers, as if to calm her...

She'd just felt the way he could tame a horse... and she wanted it locked in a photograph. Serenity would be the name of the photo if it were on display in many of the ways her work was displayed all over the world.

Her camera remained in her pocket, thank the good Lord. There would be no photos of this handsome cowboy. None.

"Well, I... guess that answers my question. You probably are a wonderful horse trainer," she said, hearing the breathless sound of her words as she tried to rein in her crazy thoughts. "That's interesting how they've given you your own little area out there," she said, taking the questions in another direction. "Did you not want to tame horses at your own ranch?"

There was a look that came into his face, his expression, his eyes at that question. "I'm a man who travels rodeo to rodeo, or competition to competition. I have sponsors. Endorsements and make advertisements for them. So I stay busy, or I did until lately. So, I actually don't own my own place. I move from one friend's place to the other, doing training while I'm there. Like now. It works for me. It's just lately I've been thinking about getting my own place finally. I'm just not sure where I want to do that."

Pearl couldn't help smiling at the man. "So all this time, I mean, you travel so much, you don't have your own place? I travel a lot too but have my place." The expression on his face alerted her.

"Don't think I can't afford my own place. I'm not a billionaire like we are surrounded by tonight. But I make a good living. I can buy what I want, just haven't."

"Sorry, I don't have any business asking you such a question. Anyway, I need to get back inside. Thank you." And she meant it. "Thank you for giving me a spot to relax and to talk."

She turned to head back inside. But she looked over her shoulder. "I hope that problem with your hip gets better."

Then she walked off, leaving him standing there with a stunned look on his face. And her heart thundering.

CHAPTER FOUR

Pearl walked away from Brant, feeling oddly like she'd known the cowboy far longer than the thirty minutes they'd stood there talking.

She loved being a photographer and that was her main source of income for all the special places that hired her to take photos and decorate them like the ritzy hotels and the large offices she took to another level with their assignments. Art was what she was made for, but she loved when she was hired to do a biography that included photos. And she couldn't help but wonder what kind of story Brant's would be. Yes, she'd pulled her phone out and done a little research on the cowboy.

He fascinated her. He was wonderful at riding bulls, had won so many championships that it amazed her. But more than that, he'd been stomped horribly last year and was still walking. Still standing straight, when he wasn't outside leaning down on the second railing from the top with his weight on his right leg. Her suspicion was that he'd been trying to relieve stress or pain in his hip.

Brant Randall intrigued her, and for some reason, she knew there was a story there. She pushed that thought away. She was here to relax, not think about photos or stories. Certainly not both that had to do with a take-her-breath-away cowboy.

She spotted Dora and Hawk, as they obviously won a bid with the way she spun and he hugged her smiling sister enthusiastically.

"I guess you won a bid," Pearl said as she stopped before them.

"I did! We now have the bull that will start our small herd."

"Your sister does know cattle," Hawk said.

"Definitely. Dad and Matt both trust her to pick the best, so I'm not worried at all about whether she chose the right one for y'all to start your herd. And the auction just started, no telling what all she's going to win before it's done."

Her mind went back to Brant. No matter what you call it, the man must be good at what he does. She'd heard his name but hadn't been in the rodeo world much. Ranching and rodeo went with each other but not always. There were many opportunities out there. She'd chosen photography, Kat had chosen restaurants, and Dora—the one with the talent for the cattle industry— had chosen seashell art. She smiled, thinking about life and the different ways it could go by a simple choice.

They had been blessed to be born into a family that had a deep history and success in land and cattle. And she felt the pull of it suddenly harder than she'd felt it since she'd picked up a camera and been drawn another direction.

As her dad always said, "Just because I chose ranching doesn't mean you have to choose it." And out of all of them, it had been Matt who chose it, thank goodness. It gave them all the freedom to find what they loved and not feel guilty for no one carrying on the ranch. But, though Dora was now entering the world of house renovating and looking at the two enjoying this auction, Dora might just have entered back into the cattle business by the looks of tonight.

Then the auction continued and Pearl sat there with her family, enjoying watching the excitement of the evening. And her sweet kind sister was all business as she bought cattle for herself and her dad.

As usual it was a wonderful night and she enjoyed it very much. But of everything she saw, it was the expression on Dora's husband's face that she enjoyed the most. There was admiration, love, and joy fully exposed as he watched Dora work.

Several times, she heard him say, "Lady, you definitely know your business."

That got a grin from everyone in the family. She did. Quiet Dora always knew her business and tonight it shone. She didn't bid on everything, didn't need everything. Auctions were fun because everyone who wanted something walked away with something, even if it was a second choice. But as she stood there watching, her gaze scanned the room. Her skin tingled as her gaze met up with Brant's.

He nodded, the grin already on his face. And whether she wanted to or not, she returned the smile.

"He is a handsome cowboy," Kat said, leaning in close.

Stunned she'd been caught smiling at the cowboy, Pearl looked at Kat. "He's a champion bull rider, here doing some horse training at the McIntyres' place."

"Really, you seem to know him." There was shock and a twinkle in Kat's eyes.

"I met him earlier. Well, when I went out for a breath of fresh air, he was out there doing the same."

Kat hitched a brow. "Well, my goodness. You have met him. And it looks like he liked meeting you." Her glance went back to the cowboy who tipped his hat then looked away.

"He's a nice guy. Honestly, I think there could be a

story there."

Kat leaned back and looked at her with a shocked expression. "You do? How about a photo shoot?" She grinned and hitched a brow. "I know my sister, the photographer extraordinaire and the storyteller that finds the stories that make the magazines."

Pearl should have kept her mouth shut. "I'm here to relax, not hunt work."

"Right. I remember that now. Good luck relaxing here at home. Especially with that handsome cowboy so near."

"You need to head on back to Kona, sis."

"I am heading out tomorrow so I'll be out of your hair. But that handsome cowboy will still be around."

"Right. Don't get excited thinking you're going to get inside information on the new man in town." That got her a grin and then thankfully things got busy again and distracted Chef Kat from zeroing in on her.

She was thankful no one else had been paying attention to their conversation. She was, again, here to relax.

* * *

After the auction was done, Brant hadn't bid on anything but he'd accepted horses to break or train.

Now, he had plenty of work to do so, like Jackson had predicted, it was a good night for him.

Even during his conversations he'd been distracted by the beauty across the area with her family. She and her sister seemed to be enjoying themselves at the end, and he couldn't help smiling at Pearl when she caught him watching her.

He stood to the side, and, yes, she caught him staring that one time, and he'd smiled broadly. Couldn't help it. And this time, she smiled back. He reminded himself again that he wasn't here for anything like that. And she had said she wasn't either—they hadn't had a deep conversation about it, but it was there.

He'd gone back inside, putting distance between him and his thoughts about Pearl. Soon, he had several more horses to train. He was stunned, but Jackson had told his friends that he was staying on the ranch and going to train some of the horses.

Train some, break some. Even a broken horse needs some work sometimes. So he and his back had a defined schedule of things to do. Everybody came back inside, and he told himself he should head on back to his cabin. He had work to do tomorrow, and he didn't need to be distracted by the elegant Pearl.

But the moment she walked in the door, he was totally and completely stuck in place. Something about that woman dug deep and as the music started for the dancing and celebrating of the night he knew he wanted to ask her to dance. But he wouldn't.

And he didn't. He stayed on his side of the room talking to cowboys and noticing that Pearl smiled at each cowboy who obviously asked her to dance but she never took to the floor with any of them.

As he watched her turning down requests for dances, he assumed, cowboy after cowboy until finally, midway through the first dance, the cowboys had given up or had gone and gotten somebody else to dance with. And there she stood beside her sister. Those two hung out together all the time, it seemed.

But then the sister accepted a dance offer and left Pearl standing there as Kat was swept away into a slow dance with the cowboy. The song was halfway over by the time he made it across the room. Yeah. His boots had done the walking, and now as he stopped in front of her, he had to do the talking. "Hi," he said softly.

Her gaze was on him as if she had watched him cross the room. "I'm assuming you saw me say no to dancing since you were standing across the room there and could see."

He grinned. "I noticed. So, I guess you saw me not dancing since I was standing across there and you were watching me."

"I wasn't watching you," she denied. "I just caught sight of you a few times. We are or were standing almost straight across the room from each other."

He grinned. She had been watching. He liked it a lot, whether he wanted to like it or not. "I see you've said no a lot of times. You sure know how to disappoint cowboys."

She grinned now. "I do not. I just don't want to dance. And neither do you, obviously."

"I hadn't really planned on it, but here I am."

"What do you mean, here you are?"

"I mean, here I am. I'm asking you to dance."

She was stunned—her expression told how much. "Do you like rejection?"

He laughed, couldn't stop it. "No. Actually, I'm not used to rejection, but I figured if every other cowboy in this building got told no, I could get told no too. Or maybe… I'd be the one who would get the dance."

They stared at each other as the song came to an end. She hitched her pretty lips up on one side. "Well, there. That solves the problem. The song is over. So no one will know you don't have to be rejected. No one has to know you were asking me to dance."

He felt the surge of challenge that he got before sliding onto the back of a bull. The challenge always had him focusing. This time it was on getting her onto the dance floor. The music started again, "*In Case You Didn't Know*," the soft lyrics rang out from the singer.

"I'm actually a Brett Young fan and *In Case You Didn't Know*, is a touching song. We should dance to the title so people will stop looking at us." He lifted his hand to the challenge. "Why don't we dance?" Though he didn't want to, he felt every word as he turned his hand so that she could slip hers into his. He waited, then added, "I guess you can say I like the challenge."

Her eyes twinkled and then she placed her hand in his. "I do too."

Her hand in his was like a lightning bolt, it struck him hard as he closed his fingers around hers. Then feeling the beat of the song he tugged her close, looked deep into her eyes as he felt the rapid beating of her heart against his heart. Just for a moment he let that feeling take over then he spun her away with the beat of the song. The lady had the grace of someone who knew how to dance as their fingertips remained touching and then he pulled her back, and together they began two-stepping to the music.

It had been a long time but Brant was suddenly a happy man and for the moment his back wasn't hurting at all.

Her gaze locked on his. "This was just a challenge and I took it just like you thought I would."

He grinned. "I have a feeling that the world-renowned photographer likes challenges." He twirled her again, pulled her back into his arms. Her body bumped against his and then she was back in step with him.

He didn't hold her close like he could have, like he wanted to. He let her have her space.

"Yes. I do like challenges. And I have a feeling that there's a story in you."

That took his breath away in a different way. "What do you mean by a story in me? No articles. No stories."

Her lip hitched. "So that answered my question. There is a story."

"I thought you were a photographer."

"I am and an article writer. I haven't written any novels. I like stories that are true and have meaning in them or mystery or just plain draw. And I'm not sure of all that which one you are, but I mean, you are a champion bull rider who can still walk straight up. Hurts sometimes like when I met you a while ago, but you took it and now you're out here dancing."

He spun her again, while his brain worked through what she'd said before he pulled her back into his arms. And this time, he looked down into her sparkling eyes. "I'm here to train horses and take a break from bull riding."

She nodded. They were close. So close. He was still holding her next to him. He could feel her heart beating, and it was thundering just like his.

"There is a story here. You're just not telling me."

The song came to an end and they paused, still connected, still gazing into each other's eyes. And more than not wanting to tell her what his life was about right now, Brant wanted to kiss Pearl.

"I think I better let you go now, or rumors will start about Pearl McConnell and the bull rider. Thanks for the dance, and thanks for coming outside and talking to me for a little bit. I'll see you later."

He released her, made himself release her, then he turned and strode to the exit and out the door. This day had been nothing like what he'd expected. From the moment Pearl had entered the huge tent his world had tilted her way.

But now, with each stride he was taking his world back. He had no room for tilting toward a lady. Especially one who captured him from the first moment.

He had a life to get in order, and an interview he had to get through soon. The last thing he needed was a woman around and rumors starting.

CHAPTER FIVE

Pearl stood still and watched the cowboy stride away as he left her standing in the middle of the dance floor alone. Frustration swarmed over her, as much at herself as toward him. Standing tall, she headed toward the exit also, not following him, but leaving. It was time and she didn't want to talk to anyone at this moment. Her brain was stuck on repeat of when she and Brant stopped dancing—when all she'd wanted in that second was for Brant to kiss her.

She'd been shocked by her reaction but his reaction, leaving her standing frozen and speechless in the middle of the dance floor had been the wake-up call she needed.

What had come over her?

Never had she felt this strong pull toward a man. Stunned was a small word of expression for the overwhelming need she'd felt in that moment when she'd wanted to lean in and kiss the bull rider.

Watching him stride away with purpose in each step gave her the feeling of being bucked off a bull in the middle of an arena with the world watching. Now, kicking herself internally she strode from the dance floor, reeling from what had just happened and needing to talk to no one.

"You sure looked like you were enjoying that dance."

Shocked by her sister's voice and words Pearl looked to her side and there stood Kat. Pearl hadn't even seen her own sister, she'd been so lost in her turbulent thoughts.

Kat continued, "You two looked like you were talking hard and heavy and even flirting a little bit."

Her sister's grin was huge. "No," Pearl said, fighting back her shock at how off-kilter she was to have not seen Kat watching her. "We were not flirting. We were challenging each other, that's the right word." It sounded better to Pearl.

Kat's grin grew wider. "Challenging. I guess he doesn't know that you are an expert at being challenged."

"No. Obviously, he doesn't know that I enjoy a challenge. A challenge is what drives me." He did know, she'd proved it to him by placing her hand in his. The moment so very unwanted, she didn't want anything about Brant drawing her toward him.

"It drives me too, but not quite like it does you. I can start something just because I want to, not because I feel challenged to do it. You—I mean, you're the gal who hangs off the side of mountains to take somebody's picture just because you're not going to not do it."

"Right. It is partly the challenge that drives me." Sometimes too much, like now. Hearing Kat's words was making Pearl take the challenge Brant had unknowingly laid out between them even more seriously.

"I think that's perfect, exactly what you need. And I honestly loved seeing you out there having a good time."

"I wasn't having a good—" She paused. "Okay. I did enjoy the dance, but that's it for me tonight. I'm heading in. It's been a lovely night. But, a long day." And it had been, counting her flight. "When are you flying out?"

"Early in the morning. So, I guess I'll see you when I get back. Don't go crazy, but if there's a little romance that ends up happening, let me know."

"Sister, go get on your plane and head on out. There's no romance going on. I just danced with the man because... like he said, I hadn't said yes to anyone else. And when he held his hand out, it definitely was as if he challenged me, and I took the challenge."

"There you go. Everything has to start somewhere, or so I've been told."

Pearl wanted to give her grinning sister an elbow in the ribs. "Nothing is starting."

"Okay, I'll shut up before you elbow me. I'll see you later. Love you lots, sis."

"Love you, too. You be careful and have fun on your trip." Pearl gave her sister a tight hug, oh how she loved this free-spirited lady. They released each other then she headed out of the tent. Freedom surged over her as she reached the moonlight sparkling over the parking area. She took her keys from the young attendant, telling him she'd get her car, no need for him to retrieve it for her, then she headed toward her silver SUV trying to ignore the feeling of disappointment that Brant wasn't standing there waiting for his ride to be brought to him—or for her to come outside.

What was she thinking?

Shoving all thoughts away, Pearl strode to her car. Tomorrow was a new day. And she was so ready for that. This one had been totally not what she had imagined.

* * *

Three days after the dance and Pearl was at her home overlooking the beach, having coffee on the deck, feeling happy she was here. The view of the ocean water rolling in then retreating was relaxing. Thank goodness she was back to normal.

She'd spent some time at Dora's place and Matt's, glad to see them and their spouses in their own spaces. She loved how content they were and at peace. She was happy this morning too, just to sit and drink her black coffee by the sea alone as she was deciding what her next steps would be while home. She wasn't sure, and hadn't taken time off in so long she almost didn't know how to make herself just sit and relax. Knowing she was going to take time off for a day or two was one thing but not being sure what her next steps were, was starting to drive her a little crazy—the jingle of her phone's ring flowed with the tide giving her something new to think about, so Pearl picked up the phone, recognized her agent's number.

"Good morning, Pearl. How are you doing out there on the lonesome coast of Corpus Christi Bay at the gorgeous Star Gazer Island?"

Pearl smiled at the sound of Mindy Nelson's voice.

The fun lady always teased her about not ever being home. "Well, it's as good as you kept telling me when you pushed me to sometimes take some time off. I'm glad I listened to you, Agent Extraordinaire," she teased back at Mindy with her nickname. "The auction that brought me home was three nights ago and it was perfect." It truly was, she just pushed the handsome bull rider's face out of her mind as it popped up—actually hadn't dissipated from her mind all night long. She'd just been forcefully ignoring it this morning.

"I'm glad. You did need a break; your work is always outstanding and of course I call with new offers because of it."

"You have an offer?" She was blessed for her work to be wanted so much that she didn't have to advertise for work. She just had to pick from the choices. And to have time off she'd turned a lot of work down already.

"Well, I actually do—though I know you don't want it right now this is an opportunity I had to run by you."

Her excitement in her tone intrigued Pearl and she sat straighter in her chair, put her coffee down. "What is it?"

"You know that I follow rodeos. Have an infatuation with bull riders especially and what drives those men, young and older, to get on one of those powerful works of God and risk their lives for eight seconds of excitement."

Pearl did know this about her agent. The woman was from Rhode Island, not many bull riders from there but she was infatuated with Texas and other states that had a lot of rodeos going on. Pearl on the other hand suddenly had a sinking feeling take over as her thoughts went to Brant Randall.

And right on target her agent said his name.

"Brant Randall, the amazing record-breaking bull rider, is out there on the McIntyre Ranch. He's set to have a big interview and camera time next week."

"Really, I didn't know that but he was actually at the celebration the other night, and I met him." She did not say that she danced with him and still hadn't recovered.

"Well, awesome! That's good news. Here is the deal, the cowboy has an incredible story, a life story that draws fans. But lately he's disappeared. There is the contracted magazine interview and photo shoot that he's set to do next week with a top magazine."

"That's good," Pearl said, knowing something was up or she wouldn't be getting this call.

"The columnist had an accident, is okay but can't

do the interview and since you're there I was able to get the job for you if you want it. It's an awesome opportunity and you can do it basically from your backyard instead of across the world. It's just an expanded interview, you know, and photographs, which you're excellent at. And it gives you even more of an expanded market for your work. The world is infatuated with this handsome, rugged bull-riding cowboy."

She totally understood their feelings. "I'm not sure—" she said but Mindy interrupted her.

"There are rumors that he's been injured or that something is wrong and he may be on the verge of stepping out, retiring. But there is more, the man owns no home of his own, which everyone finds extraordinary or even more infatuating, and wonders why. Would you want some work while there in your hometown?"

Pearl was flabbergasted by the entire conversation. "Actually, he's here training horses, not riding bulls at the moment," she said. "And I think they were talking about it after he left the thing the other night. All the cowboys, around my sister and brother-in-law and my brother, they were all talking about how several of them hired him to tame their horses. And, well, he's evidently extraordinary at that also. So maybe he has another thing on his mind other than letting a bull buck him off and stomp all over him, crippling him for the rest of his life." The thought had her sitting straight. "He's a very smart man." He was and she knew it. Her mind instantly went to the way he'd been leaning on that fence when she'd walked out that door the night of the auction. That had been pain she'd glimpsed for a short moment before he'd hidden it.

She suddenly had a bad feeling that maybe Brant did have a problem.

"As usual your observations are kicking in. You see the potential of this story. I'm just the agent offering you this well-paying job before it goes out to others. They really want you for it though, just so you know. His life has a touching story and I think done right, it could be an uplifting story. Really, think about it, he's a famous bull rider and mind-blowing horse tamer or horse whisperer as I've heard men called. I, as a fan, am infatuated already now knowing he's a horse whisperer too."

Pearl's mind was whirling with thoughts. "Okay. I can't help myself. You know me, and you're using the fact that you know my curiosity and my infatuation with finding good stories that usually have to do with people in other states, other countries. But this is an intriguing cowboy in my own backyard. And I'm supposed to be here resting, enjoying my family… but I already know

I'm going to get bored sitting around. So, my irritating, head-thumping agent, send me all the information. I'll look it over. And I'll give you an answer tonight or in the morning."

"Fantastic. You're bored, aren't you?"

She laughed. "I was actually sitting here enjoying my coffee and this outstanding topaz ocean in front of me and nonchalantly thinking about what I was going to do today, tomorrow, and the rest of my time off. And now you got my brain working."

"I knew it, so glad I called. This could be a gigantic story, maybe a movie, and your creative mind is already thinking as always about the shots you'll take that will tell this story to everyone. And that is where you always shine. I'll send the info in a click of my finger on the computer in front of me. Talk to you later."

Pearl sat there with the now-silent phone in her hand as she stared out at the waves. Her curiosity was now overwhelmed about Brant. Especially thinking about him not kissing her as she'd been thinking about over the last few days, but of him leaning against that railing.

The bull rider extraordinaire had been in pain, more pain than she'd realized. And he'd hidden it for the rest of the night, even while twirling her around on the dance floor.

Her curiosity was revved, and she knew once she looked over the paperwork that she had a job. Excitement and some trepidation filled her. This could be an life-changing story—there was something about Brant Randall that was undeniable and she had a feeling she wasn't the only lady that felt it. Mandy could have been faking her excitement to get her into the story but Pearl didn't think so.

Relief came over her in that moment that maybe what she was feeling was normal for everyone when they were around Brant.

No, she knew it wasn't so, but it helped ease her tension a bit.

A tiny bit.

CHAPTER SIX

"Look. I know Charles was going to do the story on me. Charles, the guy I know and okayed the interview with." Brant stared at the horizon as his agent talked to him on the phone. "I agreed to the story only because I know Charles and trusted him." The story was going to be about the champion bull rider who had taken a leave, and everybody suspected he was quitting. But this was supposed to be an article on successes that he had made, inspiration that he was, and he liked to be an inspiration to young boys, young men, and women, girls who wanted to enjoy the fun, excitement and challenge in the rodeo arena. It drove him. Always had. He loved it. Now he was struggling to tell it goodbye but needed to walk away.

This interview was his closing of that chapter in his life. Now, with Charles out and some stranger stepping in, he wasn't sure he'd do it.

He was a bull rider who was hurt, who knew if he wanted to walk when he was older and not struggle because of more injuries he needed out now. And then, if he ever decided or met a woman whom he wanted to marry, then have kids and enjoy playing with his kids, this was the time to start a new life that didn't include bull riding. Even later in life if he wanted to be able to bend down without trouble and play with his grandkids now was the time to make a change. Or these were things he'd never know if he continued bull riding.

He wanted a future and this interview could be a good thing. "If he can't do it, then who is taking his place? I'm here on the McIntyre Ranch. They built me a corral where I'm taming and training horses and I'm ready when you send the man my way."

"They have someone there in Star Gazer who can take over the story, and you may have already met her."

Her. His curiosity spun suddenly. "Who is it?" he asked though he thought he already knew.

"Pearl McConnell, the fairly famous photographer who also does reports and articles."

"Pearl McConnell?" he asked, his heart stampeding through his insides. In his brain, all he could think about was holding her in his arms and dancing with her. It had been staggering… incredible.

"She's there, and she is an outstanding article writer and photographer. Honestly, you couldn't ask for anyone better. Not even Charles, I'm sorry to say. We reached out to her agent this morning. She liked the idea and is running it by Pearl as we speak. We think the world will want to know what Pearl's going to say about you. Her agent and we think a lot can come from this."

Brant's thoughts spun out of control and he had to rope them and pull them in. Tame them down like a wild horse.

Spending time with Pearl would be hard with the way he reacted to being near her. But was it one he could deal with, *wanted* to deal with? He was here to get over a lower back problem and to start a new life. And he was overly attracted to Pearl.

The woman's name fit her because she was like a calm jewel that had pulled him in at the auction from across the room.

The first moment he'd seen her, he couldn't look away and then their gazes locked, and possibilities overtook him for a moment before he turned and headed the other direction.

Exactly what he needed to do now. But this was business, and with him starting a new business, it was important to get his name out there so this was a very important interview.

He leaned his head back and let emotional thoughts roll away. "You're right, I'll do it if she says she wants to."

"I just got the agreement email as we were talking. She's in."

"That quick?" He was shocked actually.

"Her agent was pretty sure she'd agree. She's there to take time off, spend time with her family. But, her agent said the writer in her, the creative mind that drives the woman, more than likely, would not let this story go because, well the rumors that there might be more to your story than meets the eye."

He rubbed his fingers on the tense portion between his eyes.

Yep. There was more to his story than met the eyes of everyone and he could keep what he wanted to himself. Beautiful Pearl would know only what he wanted the world to know. And if he could tame a wild horse he could tame his attraction to her that was raging through him now.

"I'm in."

"I'll get the contract to you soon. After she's written the article, which shouldn't take too long, then you can get back to training horses and taking care of all the calls you should get to hire you for more. Or, to train others with the amazing skills I've seen that you have."

That was his other thought, not just taming horses but helping others stay on the back of a bucking bull if they were driven like he was. He'd been driven and needed the bulls and there could be others out there just like him.

But he focused on his back injury as he hung up. He had to get his strength back in his hip and back in order to have the future he dreamed of… a future of family he'd never had growing up but wanted now if he could just let go of a past that held him in.

* * *

Excitement and trepidation filled Pearl as she headed out from Star Gazer Island inland toward her family ranch that wasn't near the water but in the vast land of Texas that spread out with huge acreage. Theirs and the McIntyres' and the Monahan Ranch and several other big ranches, whose owners had been at the auction.

When she drove up the long lane to the huge barn, her brother, Matt, strode out the double door. He'd told her when she called that this was where he would be, not at his house overlooking the ocean. Matt loved their ranch, with its valleys and open pastures and a bit of ocean too. He loved and was a born rancher knowing anything and everything that had to do with raising cattle and horses.

She loved everything about the views. It was all very photographic. Photography, not ranching, drove her. And today she needed a distraction as she gathered her wits about her and the interview she'd be doing. So, she'd called Matt and he'd said, "Come on out and I'll have a horse ready for you."

She was going to spend time taking new shots of their land. And if the call came through, the call that caused a tension inside of her that she was to do the job of interviewing her new neighbor and dance partner, the thought clung to her tightly whether she wanted it to or not. How it had felt to be in his arms three nights ago. Pushing the thoughts away she climbed from her SUV and smiled at her grinning brother.

"I already got your horse ready. You just be careful out there, Miss-Photographer-Extraordinaire."

She laughed. "I'm just Pearl, your odd sister whose eye catches things that people want to see whether they know it or not."

He gave her a hug. "Yes. You are like our mother. She knew a gem and I need to tell you my sweet wife loved watching you enjoy yourself the other night at the auction. Said you had a dance, an intriguing dance, before you left. Said you looked like you enjoyed the dance wholeheartedly."

"It looked like you two enjoyed it too," she said, trying to take the focus off of her.

"Yes, we did. I get the hint to keep my business mine and you keep yours yours." Her smart brother waved toward the stunning chestnut toned horse standing saddled at the gate. "I see you have your saddlebag of supplies, and I've saddled Sundial for you; she's waiting and ready. Call if you need anything."

"I will. Love you, brother."

"I love you too, sis. Now go have fun and relax. You need it. I looked at all those pictures you took in Italy, and some of them look like they put you in really, really dangerous situations."

She grinned. "Some, but you know me, I love dangling from a line out of a chopper to get a shot or from a mountainside."

"I know danger thrills you but promise me that out here on your own you'll rein in that creative, dangerous mind of yours."

"I promise."

"That gives me relief." He turned and headed back inside and she headed to the horse.

Freedom waited for her on the back of that horse riding through their property. And even for a minute today she needed that. She was a good rider, and was in the saddle and headed out within moments.

Waving at her protective brother who had once again stepped into the sunlight to lift a hand as he watched her head out. Her protective brother, the one that she, Dora, and Kat had had to step in and give space when he went through the loss of his loved one. But he was all well and happy, and she loved it.

They all knew when to give space and he realized today she needed it. As she rode, she looked up at the blue sky and the clouds and the birds flying above. Soon she was reaching for her camera in her saddle bag and pausing to take pictures without getting out of the saddle. It was just what she needed.

Then her phone rang. She let her camera hang from its strap around her neck and pulled her phone from her shirt pocket. It was her agent.

"You got the job big time. They're excited to have Pearl McConnell, extraordinaire, do the article on Brant. This could be astounding top story and you know it too."

Her heart pounded because she did know it. "Thank you. When do I start?"

"Anytime you want. He's out there at the McIntyre Ranch, and they've let him know you've taken the job. And he said that would be good."

Pearl's thoughts jumped back to the dance and the want to kiss him. She wondered if that was something he was thinking about too. She would have to put up roadblocks. Roadblocks in work that she never crossed. This was business. And when business came into play, her entire mindset changed. She would not think about nearly kissing him or the want to do it. No, not happening. This was now about telling a story made from photos and questions that would let the world know who the man was that the magazine company was paying big dollars to her for the interview.

She would give them what they wanted. That was her job and her need of adventure. This was just the first time she'd ever felt a draw toward her target like this.

CHAPTER SEVEN

Brant was in the arena working a horse and waiting for Pearl to arrive. He'd thought about her ever since he'd danced with her, and now he was waiting for her to interview him.

She'd called and told him she'd accepted the job and they set up a meeting for today. Now he saw her deep red SUV coming down the lane. She'd told him what she'd be driving and now, dirt from the road flowing in a mist around it, the red suburban came his way.

Business. That was what this was and he'd gotten up early as usual, put on his well-worn jeans, his faded denim shirt, his boots and spurs, and was ready. Though he didn't need them. He did not train a horse with spurs.

It was just a habit. Cowboys liked spurs and he was a cowboy, heart and soul—but bull rider most of all. And that was what this was all about, moving forward.

That was the story that needed to come from this interview, a story of moving forward no matter what life throws your way. He was a professional at that and he could do this. Move forward one more time but this time thinking about his future not just making a name for himself and a way of wiping away bad memories.

What kind of story was this woman going to come up with? He knew with other interviews he had some control, knowing the interviewer could use his words, but also could be creative in how they wrote things. And that was normally not a problem, he was sure of what he said. However, the moment Pearl stepped out of her SUV his pulse spiked and he knew he was going to have trouble. He'd never reacted to a woman, much less a reporter like this by just being near this lady. He forced his gaze from her to his horse.

This beauty he could control, it just hadn't learned that yet. He spoke quietly to the untamed horse, it had just reached the point of standing still at the end of the rope. "I'll be back. You just take this time to learn to be calm and wait." Using the long, flexible pole he used to train the horses with, Brant touched the horse's left hip and the horse moved slightly away. Just what Brant wanted it to do. This was a gentle way to get the horse to respond to being touched or startled and to react calmly, not erupt into kicking and bucking.

Brant tied the lead rope to the pole in the center of the arena, which would give the horse space to walk in a circle. He'd learned to do that with his own life and conflict so he understood the taming of a horse in many ways that most didn't know. Turning away he strode calmly with firm steps toward the breathtaking lady who was now walking toward the fence.

He kept his shoulders back, his steps steady, and his gaze on her, making sure nothing gave away the fact that this woman shook him up. In a good way or a bad way he wasn't sure. "Good morning," he said with a firm, but calm-sounding voice. "I see you made it okay."

She smiled as she placed a hand on the iron fence. "I did. It's a little bit of a drive on dirt roads through the ranch, but only a few miles further down the main road from ours."

"Right, I've seen the entrance when passing by." Small talk was all he had for the moment. The lady was a beauty and he was getting the feeling like he did when he started training a horse. The feeling of what was between them and how did he need to address it.

"Looks like you're training already." She focused on the horse, putting his mind on business where it needed to be.

He glanced over at the stud that was watching them. "I am. I start at daybreak. When the sun comes up, I'm out here. Sometimes when the sun goes down, I'm still here, depending on what my day is, what my horses are like, and how I'm feeling about it."

She didn't smile, just tilted her head slightly as her gaze met his. "Your work challenges you, I see."

"Exactly. Does your work challenge you?" He had a feeling it did.

"Yes, yes it does. I love a challenge."

He smiled. "I do too. Is that why you took this job?"

She gave a half grin. "In part. I wasn't expecting it. But, I'm curious, especially after our meeting the other night. What is your story?"

He hitched a shoulder, not focusing on their meeting but on what they were doing standing here right now, trying to ignore the draw that was taut between them. "Not much of a story. I can give it to you in five minutes and then you can head on out."

She laughed, literally laughed. "Right. I've taken this job and plan to do what I do and that means give it my all. Like you do when on the back of a bull and probably there in that pen with the wild horse."

They stared at each other, tension and attraction radiating between them. He fought to ignore the attraction but admired her spunk for her work. "I started

68

riding early, came out here at five this morning and have been known to start earlier. Sometimes depending on the horse, I keep going through the night."

"Really?"

"Really, whatever it takes for that horse to know we're going to make it to an understanding between us."

"An understanding?"

He nodded. "Yep, the horse has a mind of his own and a fighting spirit, at least the ones I tame. I've got the same spirit and so, we have to meet in the middle. It benefits us both and those who own the horse."

"When did you start bull riding, not training?"

"When I was twelve. The guys I'd gone to the place with were all older than me and couldn't ride the bull, so I hopped on, rode it, and I was hooked."

Shock filled her eyes. "You started riding bulls that early? I mean, is that normal?"

"There's not much that's normal in any situation like this. For some people, it is normal—some start early, some late. So you took the job, but you haven't researched bull riders?" He was shocked by the look on her face.

"No. I start from scratch with the person I meet to interview. It's me doing my research. It's me interviewing you for your story. I'm curious to learn it from you. Not articles written by anyone else."

He wondered if she was curious because he had shown her during that dance that he was attracted to her.

There was no way she hadn't felt that intense feeling that he had had to kiss her during that dance before he'd walked away. Before he had messed up. He wouldn't mess up again. "I think we need to set up some boundaries before this starts."

She nodded. "I think that'd be good. Although, I already know my boundaries. This is a business deal."

"Yes it is. I'm here riding a horse every once in a while for relief from the stress of being in a pen with a bull. I train horses and I'm good. I train them nice and calmly. And you need to know that. When you're here, you can't get hysterical. You can't go screaming or making loud noises."

"You don't think I'm going to do that, do you?"

"No. But I'm just clarifying exactly how I feel about things so that you can't say I didn't warn you. Also, you'll see I work with several during the day that are untrained, so never come inside the fence unless I tell you it's okay."

"You might remember I come from a ranch family."

"Right, but it's my responsibility right now to make sure we understand each other on these important points."

"I understand. I might not be as quick as you to get out and I get it. Believe me, my dad was the same way. My brother too."

"Quickness on your feet and watchful eyes after you are off of the back of a bull is important. The last thing you want to do is to get stomped on by a bull. Now, if you get thrown off by a violent one, it's not totally in your control whether you get stomped on. Then it's up to the clowns if they can do their job, if they can get to you soon enough."

"What if the clowns don't do their job?"

"It comes down to me, and I'm the one who put myself in the ring, not the clown."

"You are one who takes full responsibility for things."

Her words reached through the guards he held up around him. "Yes, in everything."

They stood there, stillness surrounding them.

"When am I supposed to be coming to start the interview," she asked, breaking the silence, the draw holding them there.

"I thought you already did."

"Maybe, but you're in a pen with a wild horse. When can I officially start the interview?"

"I don't care. You have to tell me how long it's going to be."

She looked thoughtful. "As long as it takes for me to get a story that jumps into my brain and makes sense."

"You mean you're going to be hanging around a lot?" This wasn't what he'd expected.

She hitched a lip. "Actually, yes. Every little thing we say and do counts."

"How long could that take?" He didn't know if he could hang out with her for a long time and not give in to the temptation to ask her for a date. A date for the cowboy that knew for some reason a date with Pearl would be a serious step for him. Everything about her told him he better be sure and be ready to step into his future if he tested the waters surrounding Pearl.

"Two or three weeks is usually what it takes for me to get the feel for the story. And then the pictures, but that's where some of the storytelling comes in. I'm not just going to take your picture when you're dealing with a horse in a pen. I'd like to ride with you out over the land. Your fans will want to see you out of the arena too. They'll want to see you in places you love here on this ranch."

He frowned. "This isn't my ranch."

She cocked her head to the side. "I know that but are you saying you haven't ridden around this ranch and found favorite spots?"

"I have been to certain areas on this stunning ranch that I ride to. Find peace at."

"That's what I want to see. It will take at least a few days riding together, asking questions and taking pictures on sunny days for me to get the feel for the article. Your readers are going to want pictures of you on a stormy day."

He felt stormy on the inside right now. Readers or not, there was no denying that the attraction he felt toward this woman could break him.

It wasn't a feeling he was used to, and not sure he wanted.

CHAPTER EIGHT

The next morning, Pearl arrived at Brant's cabin. And as she expected, he was standing outside the barn with two saddled horses waiting. They had set up a time before she'd left yesterday so today was their official first day together as… Her first official day on the job. He was her job and she was actually looking forward to it.

She climbed out of the SUV, grabbed her photo bag then walked toward him and the horses. "Good morning. I guess we're ready for a great day?"

He shrugged. "If that's what I'm supposed to say then, sure. It's going to be a *great* day."

She laughed. "I know, I know, you're not looking forward to having this done, but you agreed to it. I'm really confused why you agreed to it when you're not really looking forward to it. Is this beauty mine for the day?" She walked over to the slightly smaller horse.

"She's yours."

Pearl was already hooking her photo bag, which was like a saddlebag, over the back of the saddle. Every camera and lens she might need was safely tucked inside. "Let's do this." Then without waiting for him to tell her, she moved to the front of the horse and rubbed her finger between his eyes, behind his ears, and spoke softly to it.

"What's your name, handsome?"

"Oscar."

She hitched a brow. "Oscar? Okay. Well, howdy, Oscar. Are we going to have an adventure today?" The horse's tail flicked back and forth.

"That means, he's not sure."

She looked at Brant. "You gave me a horse that's not sure about wanting to go on a ride? Is that so I will have to show you my skills?"

He laughed. "No. I gave you a very safe horse. The last thing I need is for you to get hurt."

"I won't get hurt." With that, she took the reins, took two strides to the saddle, lifted a booted foot into the stirrup, then settled into the saddle. The horse took it all gracefully, didn't even flinch.

In the saddle, she looked at Brant and almost laughed at the startled look on his face.

"You look like a professional doing that."

"Thank you. I do come from a cowboy family and a large ranch, just down the road. I've been rounding up cattle all my life until I left home to be a photographer. But until then, I lived and worked on a ranch. Dad wanted us to be involved, so we worked it. I enjoyed it, just wanted more."

Brant put a boot in the stirrup then in a second he rose up and slid into the saddle like he'd been born to be a cowboy. Everything about him when it came to a horse was calm and collected and precise.

She knew why. "That horse you're riding is not tame, is it?"

He looked at her. "Nope. This is his second real ride." He patted the black stud on the neck in a gentle, soothing way. "He's doing good though. I ride them periodically, after I've got them used to carrying someone in the saddle. This settles the horse into being used to having a rider on their back. And as you can see, he took it easily."

The horse looked calm. It just did a couple of side steps, his ears laid back, meaning it wasn't sure of what was happening and ready to act if needed. She was intrigued watching him calmly on the horse. "You just cautiously wear them down? Easy like that."

"Yes, that's a way to put it. I look at it as helping them adjust to a new way of life. No, they won't be running free like the wild creature they were born to be, but they can adjust. We as humans adjust also in life. I treat them like I'd want to be treated adjusting to a new life—which I am doing. Are you ready?"

"Yes, I am."

"I've got us some drinks and snacks over here in my bag. And since we're riding out from here, there's a few places along the way for us to look at. Later, not today, but on another day of riding that you want to do, we'll load up in the truck and pull the horses in a trailer and get to a wider place that is interesting. You'll enjoy it. I actually will too, this is a special place and you'll see me enjoy myself out in the open, not on a bull or a totally untamed horse."

"That's what I want. Thanks for doing this. Because I know riding wild bulls and training wild horses is where your heart is."

"Was, with bulls," he corrected her with a look that said he was focusing on moving forward. She liked that about him and made note of it as he leaned down, opened a gate, pushed it forward from the saddle and they rode through out into open pasture.

"Riding a bucking bull is where your heart was,"

she said, couldn't help it.

He looked at her. "Not totally. But there is a need for speed in my life but something similar."

She laughed. "I get it. Instead of hopping in a race car and driving high-speed down the road, you hop on the back of a bucking bull that wants to trample you or grab you by your neck and toss you over the fence."

He grinned. She loved that grin and the spark in his eyes.

"You got me." They were riding casually through the tall grass, heading toward a hill that she couldn't see past.

"So, I'm still trying to figure out from just what we're saying and how calm and collected you seem to be, that there must be something in your past that got you on the back of that bull. Something drove you—like the need for adventure or something more."

"Something drove me, the need to get on the bull's back."

"I think there's something more."

"Look, do you want to see the land or do you want to dig deep today? If you want to dig deep today, maybe we need to get off the horses."

She met his stern look with one of her own. "No, I got what I wanted just now. Something deep inside you drives you to get on the back of that bull, and still wants to. But I also know that there's a good guy in there who likes calming things down. You needed to be calmed down because you needed to release anger inside of you?"

Why was she going deep like this right now? She didn't mean to. But the look in his eyes was driving her, yet she had to back off. "I'm pulling back, sorry. Honestly. I didn't mean to go there just yet."

He pulled up on the reins and his horse stopped walking. They made it a whole two hundred yards, maybe. "You want to get to know me, okay? For the readers. You don't want to get to know me for yourself. I get that. But today, to even things out, why don't we call it equal time? I ask you questions, and you can ask me questions. Then we can know a little bit about each other, not from what we've learned or what we've seen, but from each other. How does that sound?"

She'd stopped riding a few feet ahead of him and now looked over her shoulder at him as his words settled over her. Did she want him to know anything about her? More than she had let on the other night when they were standing by the fence line? "We opened up a little bit at the auction by the fence the other night."

"Yes, we did. But at that point, I just thought I was helping a gal that was kind of lost get through the evening. I didn't know that lost gal was going to be digging deep and interviewing me. So, how about if we start from two people on the backs of horses riding out into the pasture on a sunny day, just trying to ease the strain that's between them?"

"I'm not stressed."

"So you say. I know from the other night, something had you stressed out."

He's right. "Okay, okay. We're equal. Today it's about you ask me questions, I ask you questions. But, you can't say I can't use it. You'll get to read what I'm going to write before I submit it. How's that sound?"

He shrugged. "You're going to write what you're going to write. I don't have to read about myself."

Whoa, that was a strong thing to say for him. He'd ridden up so he was now right beside her. Her heart thundered as their gazes locked. Locked in challenge and surrender. "Right, we need common ground to start with if we're going to get to know each other."

"Exactly."

"Then it's a deal. But, just so you know, if I end up finding something out about you that you don't like, that maybe digs too deep," she almost said, 'Hurts too much'. "All you have to do is tell me not to put it in the article. It's nobody's business."

"Sure, whatever, right now, it is a beautiful day, and there's nothing like riding through a pasture of wild flowers on a pretty sunny day."

With a friend riding beside her. Friend. Olivia had ridden beside her for so many years growing up before she got ill. Pearl's heart clenched tight as she realized Brant was still watching her. Were they friends?

Could they become friends?

He was just being positive and she got that, but looking at him, she had a deep, deep feeling that they really could be friends. The meeting in the dark beside the fence at the dance resonated through her. And the feeling of being in his arms while dancing.

Pushing that thought away she nodded. "Friends riding on an picturesque perfect day. Let's go." And they did. They rode and the hilltop called to her suddenly, and with a laugh of relief she looked across at him. "Catch me if you can," she declared and tapped the horse with her boot heels and instantly the race was on as she and her horse galloped up the hill. And she heard Brant laugh then the sound of his horse charging after hers.

She laughed when he caught her on his strong not yet tamed horse that was thrilled to race free. "Hey, you didn't tell me you were going to try to escape."

"You wanted to get to know me, there you go, riding a horse, letting it run free is something I love."

They'd topped the hill on the run and he'd caught

her as they neared the bottom of the hill on the other side and a huge lake was before them. Cattle were grazing on the far side.

"Is this what you brought me to see, a lake?"

He laughed. "All ranches that have cattle or horses have lakes or ponds. We're just going to ride around the rim then go on up that trail on the other hill."

"Fine. I promise I won't race you this time, but if I don't race you, that means you have to talk, tell me a little bit about yourself. I need to know you better before I can write a book—I mean an article."

He cocked his head to the side. "I'm not worth writing a book about. Honestly."

"And you didn't give me permission to write a book about you either. I'm just doing an interview. I just misspoke." She did it because she felt deep inside the man was worth writing a book about. Why did she feel that way? "How about telling me what got you into bull riding?"

* * *

"Okay, let's just say by the time I was twelve, I was on my own. I was in a foster home but still alone in my heart and brain. Although I have to add that the foster home and couple who ran it were nice. They did their job, but when you—" He paused, stopped talking as that time rushed back to him. *Why did I start talking about this?* "Anyway, the foster home was in the city. To cope with being there among people all new to me, I started reading and came across articles about this foster ranch for boys in Texas. It was really cool to read about and I snagged onto how they got to ride horses, herd cattle, and build fences among other things."

"Is that Sunrise Ranch in Dew Drop, Texas? And I read about one of the boys who secretly became a professional bull rider."

"Yes, amazing place. I didn't get to go there, but I thought it was cool and I started thinking about maybe looking around, seeing if I could find a place I could get sent to like that. Or at least in the country. I was hard to live with, had a lot on my mind that drove me, still does. I needed space and I didn't communicate well. Because of that, I didn't have to worry too long about being in town because I got switched from one house to a different one. This one was a little bit further out in Texas, and it was out on a farm."

"Just like you wanted."

"They didn't have any horses or cows. But, like before a nice lady ran it and let me have some freedom to roam the land. Down the road, through the pasture, there was a round pen on the place connecting to my foster home and some guys liked to try and ride bulls."

"So you got what you wanted." She was hooked on his story now, wanted more than anything to find out about what put him alone in the world and drove him to the back of a bull.

He didn't say why, but she had a feeling it was because he was angry. That he needed to be on the back of that bull. And she realized as she looked at him, she really wanted to know everything about this man, not just for the article but because… she needed to know.

CHAPTER NINE

The woman was driving him crazy as he rode through the pasture away from the lake. He was taking her to a scenic, peaceful place, a place that Jackson had told him about when he'd first arrived at the ranch. He purposefully didn't talk anymore for a while. Thank goodness she rode beside him silently also. He knew, like he'd known when they booked this, that it would go deeper than he probably wanted it to, that it felt like he could control what he didn't want to say but for some strange reason, when talking to Pearl, he wanted to talk.

He wanted to know her thoughts.

He wanted to open up, and for him, that was highly unusual.

"Oh my goodness. It's beautiful," she gasped.

Her words beside him struck a chord in him. "That's what I thought the first time I saw it. It's a awe-inspiring lake." It was surrounded by rocks, rocks that were nice to sit on while you were thinking, contemplating your day, your year, your life. Jackson had needed it. And for some reason, the man knew that he needed to come here too.

Why he decided to bring Pearl here—because she'd wanted to see something that meant something to him. It did, but her words, for some even stranger reason, made it mean more to him.

"It's beautiful, isn't it? Peaceful," he said. "Do you want to get off the horse and sit a while?"

She looked at him. "Sure. It draws me it's so outstanding. We have beautiful places on our land too, but that's what's unique about land, they all have their special places. You come here to think, don't you?" she asked.

He dismounted, reached for her horse's bridle as she did the same. Then he tied the two horses to a tree. They weren't going to go anywhere anyway. They would just stand there and graze, but it didn't hurt to be careful in case something spooked them, especially his horse. Standing by the tame horse he'd given Pearl was another reason he'd brought it, because the very calm horse could help teach the wild horse how to stand beside each other.

As he led the way toward the flat rock, his brain told him to be calm around this woman. Two people, one needing to be calm—his heart pounded, rhythmic beats as he stepped up onto a big rock. He reached back and held his hand out for her to slip hers into. When she took his hand electricity ignited through him.

No way could he deny in that moment that there was something about this woman that caused feelings to ignite through him that he'd never felt before.

Not going there. She stepped up and was now standing beside him, standing close, looking up at him. So close—*don't go there.*

He stepped back, still holding her hand as he moved to the edge of the rock, dropped to one knee, and then on his hip then he was sitting on the rock. He still held her hand making sure he had her as she took the spot beside him. Instantly, she pulled her hand from his.

And why not? She was safely seated and taking the responsibility from him. "I love the sound of water rippling. And this one is peaceful."

"Yes. It is," he agreed, looking at the water and not at her. "It's got a way of calming you."

"That's what I thought. And I have a feeling when you first came here, you really needed to be calm. I know we're not getting into it, but you knew when you first came here that you needed to get out of bull riding and go into horse training. The calm world of horse training even though, as I suspect, you chose horse taming but would still prefer riding a bucking bull. Bulls don't need to be calmed down. They're wild. You learned to be a bull rider because you needed it, right?"

So here they were again. He gave in. "Yeah. I needed to be on the back of the bull. I didn't just want to ride it. I needed to be there. At the age of twelve, I had so much infuriation raging through me, anger. It tore me up inside, and I needed a release. People didn't want to be around me. I was ornery. I was quiet. I kept to myself. I made it hard. But the moment I got on the back of that bull, I rode my first one past eight seconds, and it gave me a relief I had needed for five long years."

The rippling of the water as it met the creek bed and headed down creek filled the silence. "Do you still need that? Are all these years since you were six, seven? Have you found peace from whatever it was that caused you to be like that?"

His heart ached. He hadn't wanted to go here, but here he was. "Yes. I've come to deal with it. I've learned that some things aren't your fault. You can't blame yourself, but if you can't stop it, that stays with you. Knowing that if you'd have just woken up, if you'd have just been stronger, you could have stopped it. I was six years old and wasn't able to help."

"I can't help but ask what happened to you? I'm so sorry. I can tell it was life-changing. Only tell me if you want to. Need to."

"I was six and asleep upstairs. My parents were asleep on the first floor and the furnace caught fire. When I woke up, my dark room was full of smoke. But, I made it to the door but it was so hot and the smoke was overtaking me. I was young but made it back to the window and climbed through and onto the tree limb that I was known to climb out on. I made it down the tree easily, even as horrified as I was because I was a born tree-climbing kid."

"I'm so sorry."

"When I made it to the ground my room caved in, so I barely made it out. I still can't figure out how I was able to breathe. They told me later that my mom and dad probably suffocated from the smoke before they woke up. Before they burned. I can't decide whether I need to be thankful for that because they didn't suffer or be angry because they didn't wake up and have a chance to get out. The only other person I'd had to love was my grandmother, and she'd died the year before so I was now alone. I had no one."

"That anger drove you to get on the back of bulls."

He nodded. "Yes. Still does. I understand that at

six, there was probably nothing I could have done for my parents. Even if I had made it downstairs to them, they were probably already gone. And I probably wouldn't be sitting here today, a champion bull rider, talking to a lovely woman, sitting by a lake, listening to the gentle flow of the water." It was true, still to this day his heart ached. He saw the tears in her eyes. He thought about his grandmother and her pearl necklace that she'd left him. It had perished in the fire but Pearl's soft look had him thinking about that sweet time with his grandmother.

"I'm so sorry." Her voice wobbled as she wiped her eyes then looked out across the lake. "I feel your pain. You never forget those you've lost. I know, everyone loses someone sometime." She paused.

"As an adult I understand that. Another reason I'm leaving bull riding behind. I want to be able to enjoy a family if I ever decide to look for love."

"That would make your parents happy." She smiled at him and his heart stumbled inside his chest. "And also some fan out there if she were able to win your heart. You have so many fans."

He frowned, not wanting to go down this trail. "How did we get to this?"

"You started it, talking about realizing you might want a family." She placed a hand on his arm, sending instant fire blasting through him. "Don't worry. I won't be putting any of this in my article. But it gave me more insight into who you really are, Brant Randall." Her gaze dropped to her hand on his arm and he saw her expression tighten before she let go of him.

"So," he said, focusing on where they'd been before she'd touched him. "Did you move forward to fulfill the things Olivia wanted you to fulfill?"

"Yes, like I said before, taking photos was my calling and she knew it and encouraged me."

"You travel the world, making people happy who see your outstanding photo art and articles you write. The reviews say only good things about the photos I've seen."

"You know my work?"

"I did my research when I found out who was interviewing me. I needed to know who was going to be talking to me and writing about me. And, I also needed to know who I'd been talking to that night at the auction. I saw you started with ocean photography, which you did off the shores of Marathon in the Florida Keys. Read that you jumped into taking photos underwater." He was fascinated with her story, and enjoying talking to her. No matter what happened he was glad he'd agreed to take a ride with Pearl. Even if he was having to adjust to the way the woman affected him.

* * *

"Yes," Pearl said, answering the amazing cowboy's question. She had been trying to ignore the attraction she felt being near the man and was glad to have something to talk about other than the way her fingers had started tingling when she'd touched his arm. "I found my calling during happy times. I realized I was obsessed with taking photos and floored by the exposure those photos got almost instantly."

"Where do you enjoy going the most?"

"Goodness, my sister Kat loves Hawaii and my sister Dora is now learning places she'll love traveling with her husband. For me," she chuckled, "there are so many places I've been to that picking my favorite is tough. I've seen some remarkable places but I think if I really pick it would be where it all started off the coast of Marathon, Florida, riding through the waves out to the Hump."

"The Hump?"

"It's a hump deep underwater between Cuba and the Keys where so many go to fish. It's there that I got some of my first life-changing ocean photos of colorful stunning fish. The photos that got noticed."

"Do you go back there often?"

She sighed. "Actually, no, I haven't been back in a

long time. I stay so busy traveling the world, seeing places like Switzerland and Greece, those are both beautiful. But I stay busy taking photos here in America too, been to almost every state taking photos of people and landscapes I've been hired to photograph. I travel to places I explore and take what I love and believe will sell and because of that I also do a lot of commercial art. My photos are in many, many buildings."

"I saw that. I read an article about how you love doing photos that help people walk into a hospital and hopefully your tranquil photos help them calm down. Same for in a lawyer's office where tensions can be high and a tranquil piece of art can help calm them."

"Yes, that's all true. You did research me." She was shocked by his words.

"What pictures do you have in your home?"

That question shocked her. "You really are trying to get to know me, asking me these questions. I know they are to keep me from asking you questions but I agreed." She lifted a shoulder. "I have no pictures in my house except a few of my family. I go to the places I want to go and have them on my camera and files, but also in my memory. For me, when I look out my living room window and see the bay, the sunlight, the moonlight, the gentle waves of the water, it takes my mind where I want to go. I'm lucky that I travel so much that I don't need a photo. But one day... one day if I stop traveling, then I'll have plenty to pick from." Or new ones to take, right here."

"Maybe of a family you might have."

Shock washed through her. "Maybe." They stared at each other.

"I think I'd like to see some of those pictures," he said. "Visit some of those places. I've seen places while on the back of a bucking bull, but that's about it with my travels."

The way this conversation had suddenly turned, inspired her artist mind and it was working. "Do you fish? Have you ever been to the Keys?"

"I ride bulls or did. Never even thought about going to the Keys and have no idea if I'd be a good fisherman. Never tried it."

Her brain was spinning. "This article just took a detour. What if this article I'm writing could be about your new beginning, not your past. This is your step forward from bull rider to not just taming horses but helping others through your story. There are so many people out there who need to know they could start over. Start from scratch no matter how good they were at something or how bad they were at something. They might need to start fresh from a hurting heart. Or an injury. Sometimes people just need a do-over, a new beginning. You need that. I see that now. This article shouldn't be all about your bull riding career, yes, it starts there but it's about you deciding you want to get off the back of a bull and have a new adventure in life." She was stunned by her words and the excitement rolling through her.

He stared at her as if either she was crazy or maybe his heart was pounding, his brain racing just as fast as hers was. "This is crazy."

"No, this is what I do. You need to open up and feel free so you can move forward from the past of that little boy who lost his parents and the grandmother he loved. One day, you might want to have your own family, a wife and kids."

"Where are you going?" he asked, looking at her like she'd lost it.

"You're not sure about a family. I get it. I'm not either. But this isn't about me but about you." True but suddenly it slammed into her that he needed freedom from the past and she did too. That didn't mean this was about them…

"You're a good interviewer. You just hit on the thing that haunts me the most. My parents loved each other desperately and loved me too. I miss that love. But, and I think you get it, I don't know if I ever want to take the chance on losing someone else."

Pearl's heart ached but she smiled tenderly. "I totally understand. I get it. That's kind of where I am at the moment too. Olivia wanted me to have it all. I did what I wanted, and I diligently went into picture taking. That's where I thought I wanted to be, and I'm very successful at it. But now, I don't know, something in me wants to be back here, maybe looking for a new missing part of my life. Please relax, I'm not talking about you and me as a couple. I'm talking about we are kind of in the same spot of figuring out what our next step in life is. We just happen to suddenly be thrown together to maybe help each other figure it out."

Their gazes remained locked. "Maybe, you're right."

She tore her eyes from his, her heart thundering. Yes, she was attracted to the man but there was more to this. She suddenly felt a gentle peace come over her. And in that moment, she felt his hand lay down on the rock open beside hers. She looked at it and then slipped hers into his and he gently laid his fingers over hers, giving her a comforting squeeze.

Pearl felt peace roll over her in that moment and she hoped Brant did too.

CHAPTER TEN

Brant watched Pearl drive away after they'd ridden back to the barn. They'd both been speechless after realizing they hadn't just thought they had similarities in their backgrounds, but now knew they did.

Both of them were fighting some of the same emotional battles. But he was a man. That's what bothered him. He was a man. He wasn't a wimp. He wasn't afraid. He rode bulls, after all. So why, now that he looked at how he was handling what was going through him, and he looked at how Pearl was handling what she'd been through, should he have handled it in a different way?

Should he be over it? He strode back to the pen, calmly walked inside, though his insides were not calm at all.

Turmoil filtered through him like he'd been struck by violent lightning. And this was when taming a horse was as hard as riding a bucking bull, because here, he couldn't let the rage fill the pen like he could on the back of a bull.

Here, he had to move evenly as he spoke to the horse, letting the rage inside of him calm down, using his soothing words to teach the wild horse how to handle its new life.

Over the next few days that is what he did. But still, he thought about the ride with Pearl across this countryside. He was still a little confused by his emotions, but he was back to training his horses. She had told him it would be a few days before she got back. She was coming tomorrow and this morning, he was going to breakfast with Jackson.

They were heading to a small diner on the outskirts of Star Gazer Island for breakfast.

He had called Jackson and asked him to go to breakfast with him and now they took a seat toward the far edge of the diner. They ordered their eggs, bacon, sausage, and coffee and he looked at Jackson. "Thanks for coming. I needed to talk."

Jackson tipped his head to the side, his Stetson shadowing his eyes that studied Brant closely. "What's up?"

"You know I don't talk about my past often, and they're doing that interview on me. Well, Pearl is the interviewer. The other guy got sick and since Pearl is here in town, her agent booked her for it because they know what a spectacular interviewer she is."

Jackson smiled. "She's a lovely interviewer too, we saw the two of you dancing the other night. Is something going on?"

The question dug deep. "That's why I have you here. We went out for a ride a couple of days ago because she thought that would be a good way to get to know each other a little more—for the interview's sake. I took her to that lake on the property with the pretty view and we sat there and talked. Strange enough, we both have a history that in many ways parallels each other. Yes, in different ways but I hadn't realized how much she's been through until we talked that day."

Jackson put both hands around his coffee mug. "You never know what someone has been through until you talk. That's why she wanted to meet with you. When I met Nina, I had no idea what that woman had lived through, being stalked and hunted and hiding out. I'm thankful I was there for her when she needed me. She had no idea what I'd lived through when I lost my dad. It was a horrible experience. What's your experience? Is that where you're having problems?"

It was a point-blank question that Brant didn't like answering, but today, he needed someone to talk to other than the woman he couldn't stop thinking about. "Yeah." He then told Jackson about the fire. Told him how young he was when he had to make it down a tree to escape the burning house all while knowing his parents were inside. How that was forever on his heart.

Jackson looked sad. "Been there. I couldn't get to my dad when he was drowning downriver. I tried, but I couldn't get there no matter how hard I tried. And I wasn't a six-year-old. I was an adult. What I've learned, and I'm just going to tell you this, and you know it. You've been riding bulls to take your anger out, and I get that. But I'm going to say, you are an amazing horse whisperer. You know that's what you are, don't you? And you're going to work wonders."

"I know. And they listen."

"Exactly. And as good a bull rider as you are, your quiet way of training a horse is perfect and wanted. Those who can do that, stay busy. So, have a life out there that doesn't have anything to do with anger that drives you because you couldn't save your dad. I'm having a wonderful life with my family now, and I'm so thankful for this life and know my father is too. But I'm at this point. Me telling you that is all I can do. It comes down to when your heart is ready, when you're ready.

I'll add though that when the right woman comes along, the woman who needs you to be the man that you are, that needs to step out if needed, that'll wake you up."

Brant thought about that as their food was delivered. He didn't really have an appetite anymore, but he picked up a piece of toast and broke it off. "I guess it's none of my business to say that Pearl is looking for something new in her life too. She just feels it after losing her friend, Olivia. She's an amazing woman, and I don't know if I'm the right one to be in her life. But there is no denying that there is attraction."

Jackson picked up his fork, dipped it in the scrambled eggs, smiled at him. "All I can tell you, buddy, is you'll never know unless you test the waters. If you don't test the waters, you might live to regret it. I can tell you, there are plenty of cowboys in this room right now that would love to have Pearl McConnell looking their way. And if she's talking to you, that means something."

Yes. It did, and he knew it. He could tell she didn't talk to many, not about her past or hurts, just like him. "Thanks. We'll see where it goes."

And then they ate. He knew what Jackson had just said was true. There were many, many cowboys who would love for Pearl to look at them with those stunning deep ocean eyes of hers. He just wondered if when her eyes met theirs, would they have the reaction he had literally rattling him through and through.

* * *

Pearl had taken time off to start working on the article she was writing, but mostly because she needed time away from Brant. She reacted to the man like she had never reacted to anyone, and it was driving her crazy. That day sitting on that rock when he'd covered her hand with his fingers, her world had turned upside down. She'd wanted much more than just his hand, she wanted him to hug her, to hold her close, to kiss her. She was stunned by how much she'd wanted that.

In her mind, she saw what he'd been through as a young kid, the horror of it. Then he'd climbed onto the back of a bull, not because of the challenge but to relieve the stress going on inside of him. The stress he'd felt as a young kid who believed he'd failed because he hadn't been able to save his parents. Always thinking about what he could have done differently. This had to have been so hard on Brant the child.

But now he was a man, and instead of thinking about him as the man she was interviewing, she was thinking about the man she wanted to know better.

The man who stated that he wasn't sure he would

ever take the step forward of falling in love because he couldn't handle losing her. Her brother had taken that step with sweet Olivia, knowing full well he loved her with all of his heart, and knowing she was going to die. He'd taken that step forward knowing he'd rather have her as his wife for a short time rather than living the rest of his life not having said those vows.

Though Pearl knew that Olivia had not wanted him to do that, once he'd asked her to marry him, sweet Olivia couldn't deny that she wanted to be his wife. And so their love story began, a magical world that had to do with loving with all their hearts before Olivia went to heaven.

Then their story continued as her brother lived without Olivia before finding love again in a very unexpected way.

Pearl had met many people who had lost their loved ones and never remarried. And she met many who had never married, not once, and one of those was her. Was that why she was home?

Was she, Pearl, looking for love?

Love. What did it have to do with it?

Everything. That's what Dora had said. Sweet Dora. Quiet, quiet Dora. As Pearl sat there on her porch overlooking the ocean, her heart thundered thinking about knowing that kind of love. And for the first time ever, an image appeared before her, and it was Brant. *You are interviewing him not dating him*—the thought came to her like a slap in the face. This was business.

Romance was not part of the story. Her fingers tapped quickly on the arm of the chair as her brain rolled with thoughts. She wasn't the person who decided destiny. She wasn't here to decide for Brant what his destiny was to be but she knew deep inside that with the interview she could help him. She knew she could help him know that he was making the right decision giving up bull riding for horse whispering. It would help keep him safe so one day he'd be able to teach his own children how to ride horses and he'd be there with them having fun.

The thought radiated through her and a smile grew across her face and in her heart. She could help him find his new life with this interview. She could help him see there was more out there in life waiting for him than where he was. It could also help others see it in their own lives hopefully by watching him.

People could learn to deal with their problems and still have a life. No, you don't always have control of your destiny but... the writer in her was thinking. It was thinking hard. What you have control of is how you look at everything, how you deal with it.

That was what sweet Olivia had wanted her and her sisters to know, and her brother too. Olivia dealt with what was given her in a heart-touching, tender, loving way. She took it and passed her love on to them and her hope that they would take her death and live with it the right way too.

A surge of excitement pushed through Pearl and she stood up, walked to the edge of her deck. Then she walked out down the pathway that led from her house to the water. There she walked into the shallow, sandy shore as the water came in over her bare feet. Its touch instantly reminded her of the warmth of Brant's fingers as they'd covered hers, sitting on that rock watching the lake water. The connection was still with her and she knew for certain now, that before she went back out there to continue the interview she had some major decisions to make about how to carry this interview forward. What direction she wanted to go.

CHAPTER ELEVEN

"What did you say?" Brant stared at her with a confused look on his face.

She smiled. "I said that the jet is waiting, my dad's jet. To carry me and you to Key West, Florida. We'll fly to the tip of the United States, then we'll take a car and drive to Marathon over the Seven Mile Bridge. Might stop at the wonderful Bahia Honda Beach on the way or on the way back. I've booked a couple of rooms for two nights but the day after we land we'll go deep-sea fishing. I'll take you to eat the first night and then on the second night we'll go out and eat the fish you've caught at a wonderful restaurant that will cook it for us. The boat we take out and the fishing guide is excellent. I'll get firsthand information for this article for readers who love you, who are interested in you, to see your reactions to a new adventure."

"You've got to be kidding me."

She smiled. "No, I'm very serious."

The woman had a smile he hadn't stopped wanting to see again. But this was crazy and extremely unexpected.

"Seriously," she continued after he said nothing. "I know this is last-minute, but I figured if I gave you time to think about it, you'd say no. This would be perfect for the article. Just think about all the people you might inspire who are trying to decide whether they could change their life. And you're looking for a new adventure. You told me you have never been there but wanted to go someday. I can get you there and I can document it. You can tell me yay or nay on whatever you want. But I thought about it, and it won't let go. I also have to say that I could get you out there on that water and since you've never been, you might get seasick. We won't know until we're out there. No worries, if so, I won't put it in the article, we'll do something else. This is completely crazy and off the wall."

"You can say that again." It was crazy, but there was something about it and how she looked so excited about it that had Brant wanting to experience it with her.

She laughed. "I never expected this to be part of the interview. But after our talk the other day, I just can't let it go. I think your fans would love it, and you're going to have so many people rooting for you. You're going to become a very famous horse trainer. I believe that, just from what I've seen and knowing the way you are. You are a horse whisperer. I read up on horse whisperers and it is fascinating and fantastic."

"I think so, but about this trip—"

"It's going to be ideal. And with all the cowboys that lined up to give you their horses to train or break, that's a testimony right there. Believe me. These cowboys, they can hire anybody they want and they want you. They see that horse you trained winning everything it gets involved in and that's not luck. That's you. When I got offered this job I asked for control over what I wrote about in this article. And I'd really like to give you a free ride to the Florida Keys and a day of fishing for Mahi mahi. Just think how great it will be to eat it after you caught it. What do you say?"

Brant couldn't believe what Pearl had just laid out for them to do. Totally unexpected but he was still thinking about holding her in his arms at the dance and the other night holding her hand. Looking at the smiling woman right now, he realized he didn't care what they were going for, he wasn't passing this trip up. Especially after what he and Jackson had talked about. "Sure, I'm in for an adventure. So how long are we going to be gone?"

"We'll fly in today. Being here on this huge ranch, I'm sure you can have someone cover for you on feeding and whatever else they need to do while you're gone. So, we'll fish tomorrow, and then fly out the next day. Just a quick three-day trip. Two nights and one full day on the water. If we get there and you decide you need to fish more, I can stay longer. I can write anywhere." She chuckled, and he smiled.

"I can't believe I'm saying this but let's do this."

"Perfect. I've got a great fisherman who will take us to the fish. The man can catch anything. And he loves taking people fishing and teaching them how to catch them. He's a good friend of my dad's."

"What's his name?"

"Mike. And he can do anything with the boat and a fishing pole and all the gadgets that tell him where the fish are."

Brant smiled. "I guess I have to go because I need to see about this fishing. Who knows, I might decide I don't need to be a horse trainer anymore but want to become a professional fisherman?"

She laughed, her eyes twinkling in the sunlight. "We're both looking for our next step in life. I might decide to become a fisherman—I actually do love it. It is an absolutely perfect way to relax and get your mind off of anything but the fish and the topaz water."

Relaxing with this lady sounded like the best idea he'd... ever had actually. Thoughts of having a family rose suddenly inside his chest, memories of living and laughing with his parents—in that moment he saw their smiling faces. He cleared his thoughts and met Pearl's searching gaze. She was the first woman who had ever made him even think that maybe he really did want to step forward and have a family.

"You okay," she asked gently.

The woman had a way of seeing everything, catching it not just with her camera but with her fiery, penetrating blue eyes. Eyes that were set off by her almost white-pearl toned hair. He understood why they'd named her Pearl. More than that, he understood how she was so sought after in more ways than her beauty. The woman had eyes that caught everything and looked deep, wanting to catch everything... wanting to help fix it if she could.

And he was her new subject. Maybe that should bother him, but in that moment all he wanted to do was fly with her to Key West. And experience what she wanted to experience with him.

* * *

The plane had been waiting. They threw in some clothes. Pearl told Brant that if he wanted to pack some swim trunks or fishing pants that took the water, he could, if not, they had plenty of places in Key West where they could stop and pick him up everything he'd need.

"I actually don't own a pair of swim trunks," Brant said.

Pearl had smiled. "Why does that not surprise me? No worries, we'll pick some up when we fly into Key West."

They flew on the private jet her dad owned and had actually met them at their private strip and given Brant a handshake. "You're going to enjoy fishing. I do, just don't do it as much as I used to because I'm too busy traveling with my wife and having other adventures and fishing other places sometimes. Fishing gets in your blood and you don't want to let it go.

"And the guy that's going to take you out, he knows his business, believe me. He's not even what they consider a professional, but we consider him a professional because he knows where the fish are.

"Now, also, you got Pearl with you. And Pearl, she can fish just like she can ride a horse, but her love is in photography. So all I'm telling you is if y'all end up out there at the Hump, do not let her go in the water. Tie her down to the boat if she doesn't listen. It's way too deep and dangerous out there."

"I won't let her do that at all. Not with me in the boat. I mean, I agreed to go, but that's another clarification."

He looked at the now smiling Pearl. "Believe me, I only dive when I'm in safe waters, and when I have a professional team with me. I totally get it. And remember this isn't about me but you. And you're going to catch a big mahi. Mikewill find you some fish. Might find you a large school and you'll pass your limit and have to toss some back. That is my hope."

Her dad grinned. "My goodness, Pearl, I thought you were ignoring me all those years I was teaching you about fishing."

"No, Dad, no one ignores you." She kissed him on the cheek.

Brant's heart clenched at the sweet gesture, remembering his mom's gentle cheek kisses. "Thanks for the plane," he said, needing to get his memories off his mind.

"Glad to do it."

Pearl stepped toward the plane. "We'll be back and for my article my brain and my heart tell me this is going to be awesome." Then she turned and headed up the short stairs and into the plane.

Brant watched her, there was no turning back now. He looked at her dad. "I'll take care of her." And then he headed up the stairs himself. And within moments, they were up in the air.

It was a quick flight, barely three hours over the Gulf and they landed at the small airport in Key West, the end of the USA. He and Pearl had talked a lot. She'd told him stories about her scuba diving and taking photos of remarkable scenes in the water. He told her he wasn't going scuba diving no matter what she wanted out of him. But fishing was one thing.

She laughed, he loved making her laugh and he knew by the time they landed, he was probably in trouble.

But at that point, he didn't care. He wanted to see about this fishing trip she wanted to take him on. And he was curious about this article she was going to write. What in the world was she going to say? Thank goodness he got to look at the article first and take things out if he didn't like it.

Key West was a very crowded place, tiny little

roads, small but tall houses along the narrow streets. Most were one-way traffic, and lots of places for people to stay. There were a lot of people on bicycles that she had to watch out for as she drove the convertible BMW downtown. They stopped at a store and he bought some shorts and fishing attire.

Then they drove on the one-way lane out of the chaos of Key West, onto the straight two-lane road that carried them past Key this, Key that, all the little tiny islands that had the last part of their name as Key. Then they started crossing a long bridge and she took a right and drove into a small place called Bahia Honda.

"We're just going to stop and let you see it. One day if you love fishing you'll want to come during prime Tarpon time and fish there under the long bridge we just crossed."

She'd already told him that the old bridge that ran several feet from the main bridge used to be the railroad track that carried food from the mainland to Key West. Now, as they drove into the small island, the old train track was across the bay from them and looked like a broken arch, in the bay. A bay that was between the new bridge and the old unusable train track that even had pieces of metal hanging down from beneath it.

In the bay, as they got out of their car, he saw several old and new yachts sitting in the bay between the bridges.

"It's a breathtaking place," Pearl said, standing there on the shoreline where she'd led him. Standing there with her hands on her narrow hips, her eyes taking in the scene, he had to remind himself to look at what she was seeing and not at the outstanding scene she made standing there with the blue water in front of her and two bridges behind her like a frame for the picture she was in that moment.

"Yes, it is." He pulled his gaze from her and stepped to stand beside her. "So they fish for Tarpon there under the main bridge?"

"Yes, that's where it starts. Boats tie up and lines are tossed waiting for a tarpon that is traveling through here to take the bite. They are strong fish that men love to catch. This bay is where people can swim, and the water's pretty and shallow to a point. Makes a great time if some are fishermen and others like the beach. The fishermen can fish then come in from out there and have lunch at the store with the others. Makes a wonderful family experience."

He turned slightly to look at her. Couldn't help it. "You like what those people on the edge are doing." It wasn't a question but a statement.

Snorkelers were on the edge of the swimming area and he could see her there in his thoughts.

She smiled at him. "Exactly. And on the other side,

where the tide is in right now, and dirty looking. When the tide goes out it's about two feet deep for a half mile and the snorkeling is on the outer edge. For a beginner it's a nice place to experience the area beneath the water."

He nodded toward the broken bridge and the first part that was made to be a viewing point. "Have you walked up to that point?"

"Yes, it's a nice walk up the sandy hill to the concrete. Are you wanting to go there?"

"I'm more interested in seeing this Marathon you're taking me to."

She smiled. "Let's go."

They went back to the car, hopped in, and she drove them back out of the park and a few yards down they reached the Seven Mile Bridge.

He had seen the movie once that had an ending scene made here on the old bridge running beside them. "I remember once seeing the movie, and they really blew those portions of the bridge up."

Her hair was blowing in the wind as she drove, her eyes on the cars and trucks that were traveling on the bridge with them. "Yes, they blew the bridge up, but in the movie, the heroine, Jamie Lee Curtis, was caught in the huge black limousine and her hubby, who was a secret agent of some sort, saved her using a helicopter.

Fun movie. They no longer needed the bridge so why not make some money off of it?"

She continued telling him different stories as she drove the long bridge over the blue waters.

When they reached the end of the bridge she slowed to the lower speed and the two-lane road expanded to four lanes.

"This is Marathon and it's big enough to have four lanes."

He enjoyed the ride but mostly he'd enjoyed Pearl's company. She was like a walking tutorial on where you're at and what you're seeing and what you're going to do.

Marathon was a quiet town with important places. It had a hospital and schools and many, many houses and grocery stores. And an airport, just smaller than the one they'd flown into. Soon, they were turning down a two-lane road, across a small bridge with a bay on one side and condos on the other with a smaller bay behind them. They passed several streets as she drove to the street at the end of the island, where he'd realized they were at. She pulled into the drive of a large house overlooking the ocean.

She parked the car. "This actually is the place we always rent, and, no, it's not a hotel but you have space because it's big and has a great view of the bay. Come on." She got out, reached in the back, grabbed her bag, walked to the door and clicked in a combination and then opened the door.

Bag in hand, he followed her inside. Into an beautiful, large home with giant glass windows on the far wall overlooking the water. Pearl walked straight to the windows, dropping her bag on a couch as she passed it. She opened the huge glass sliding doors and stepped out onto the deck. He followed, stunned by it all.

They were overlooking the bay. "You see there across the bay, that's where we just came through. Marathon. It's much like crossing the bridge to Star Gazer Island. Looking to the right leads you to the Gulf but to the left takes you out to the open waters of the Atlantic, and that's where we'll be going tomorrow. That's our own pier where Mike will pick us up at seven in the morning."

Brant was stunned. "You definitely know your way around. This is remarkable. This is where your family stayed when you were growing up?"

She shrugged. "Yes. At least two times a year, but then, you know, my dad had been doing it forever. My mom wanted to see other places, and we were all grown up so they stopped doing it as much. All of us kids had our own lives and traveling with our business, so they sold this place."

"This house belonged to your parents?"

"Yes, but we still have access to it whenever we want it, if no one else has booked it. It's one of the more expensive homes so it's not rented out as often as all the other places, so I was able to book it for us. There are three rooms on that side, you just pick the one you want. I'll stay on this side in the master suite and we can meet in the middle in this gigantic living room. There's coffee and snacks in the kitchen. I don't know about you, but I'm hungry. Are you ready for dinner?"

Stunned was a small way to describe how he felt in that moment. "Sure. But first, let me tell you, Miss Trip Planner Extraordinaire, you are full of surprises."

He almost laughed. He had never even imagined that he would be coming on a trip like this with her. But he was ready to do whatever she wanted. Other than the article she was going to write, this was actually the first adventure he'd ever had that had nothing to do with bull riding. And he liked it.

Liked it because he was experiencing it with Pearl. Beautiful, amazing Pearl.

CHAPTER TWELVE

She drove to the main road, crossed it and they were in the parking lot of a large building with a huge straw roof that overlooked the blue ocean. She had to weave her way to the back of the long, crowded parking area that ended at a helicopter spot. She parked at the last available space and they climbed from the car.

She smiled at him as they fell into step, walking back to the straw-covered restaurant. "Yes, it is usually this busy. The food is delicious and the sunset is stunning."

"Sounds perfect." It was as far as he was concerned. They walked past a large group of people who were together and waiting on a large table. When he told them there were just two of them, and Pearl added that they wanted to be by the water at the end of the inside, the hostess smiled and instantly led them to exactly where Pearl had requested, the only table for two at the end of the outer deck.

"How is this?" the hostess asked.

"Perfect," Pearl said, smiling sweetly at the young lady, then looking at Brant.

"It is perfect. Thank you," he agreed, smiling inside and out suddenly at the smiling young lady.

"Your waitress will be here soon." Then she left and they both took their chairs and sat across from each other. He pulled his gaze from Pearl to take in what surrounded them. On his right was the rope to keep them on the deck and then the water with large fish and small fish swimming around. Across the water was a long walkway that was connected to the restaurant's outside deck up near the back of the building. There were boats tied to it, some professional boats and some that had customers walking from their boat to the end of the pier so they could come in and dine. Beyond the pier was the horizon where the water met the sky and the sun was still sitting above the line but he figured within the hour it would settle and make a breathtaking sunset.

"Sunset Bar and Grill is the perfect name," he said, looking at Pearl as she nodded in agreement. Her gaze was where his had been studying the settling sun. Now they met his and his insides rumbled with a content feeling. "I'm glad I came."

"I am too. There is a peace about sitting near the water even with the crowd around you talking."

"Yes, odd but true." People surrounding them, large groups and small groups were talking and laid back. Looking around he knew suddenly that she'd been right. "You were right, I needed a change, even if for a short time."

"You just made my day. Tomorrow will be a new experience."

He loved bulls and horses, but when was the last time he had done something different, unexpected until now?

"This is my favorite spot," Pearl said, her voice gentle as the breeze off the water. "There is nothing in our way other than the tip of the pier and when the sun starts setting the pier is an added piece to the beauty."

"Your artist's eye is always looking for that added piece." It wasn't a question, it was an observation. He was a horse trainer and a bull rider and both took a sense of skill, knowing what to look for. She was an artist through and through and everything came down to that. Even this.

Her smile spread beautifully across her delicate face. "Exactly. Before we leave, we'll walk to the end of the pier, let you get the feel of the water surrounding you."

He was enjoying the evening with Pearl and the added walk was like a topping on the night. "Sounds good to me. You definitely know your way around. This is a nice place. I like its openness, and obviously everyone does. Is it always crowded like this?"

"Most of the time and they also serve a wonderful breakfast. Though we'll have something at the house early before Mike arrives at our pier just after sunrise. We leave before they open."

"Sounds good."

The waitress came back and brought their water with lemon, asked if they wanted anything else to drink, and they both declined.

He wasn't here to drink. Didn't drink much at all anyway, and he didn't want anything to take his mind off of this moment. The moments he was spending with this woman.

The realization was like a lightning strike with a thunderstorm following it. All, telling him he shouldn't let himself even think about this woman as a date, a love interest—nothing about this was supposed to be romance. But those were the words clicking away inside his brain.

Someone important, that thought struck suddenly,

and stuck like an arrow in his heart. A turning point.

Yes, he realized no matter what happened in his life that this woman was the turning point for him. She'd seen that he needed this. His gaze was on her when she smiled, her smile bringing him back to earth instead of floating in his swirling thoughts.

"You, Mister Brant, are lost in thought." Her fingers with their clear painted fingernails, were tapping gently on the table. He suddenly wanted to lay his hand over hers and just feel the rhythm, but he didn't.

"I'm really glad you talked me into this," he said. "I mean, honestly, I never thought about needing something to break into my life and give me a little bit of a change. A new experience."

Her smile sprang to her full lips. "Awesome. Wonderful." She breathed deep, then added with soft assurance, "That's what I want. And this is the perfect place to see it happen. The Florida Keys are where the world slows down and beauty happens."

"I just arrived and already get that," he said, feeling totally relaxed. "Which makes it a good time to tell me about this article you have brewing in your mind about me. Tell me why you wanted to change it up some. Tell me more about why you're choosing this versus just interviewing me about my bull riding career?"

Her small hands clasped together on the table, and

she leaned forward. "Because, like I said, you have fans out there. Male bull riding friends and competitors who want to read about your bull riding career, learn things because you're a star bull rider. You also have young boys wanting to be like you who are watching too. But, also women and young women admiring you, some like the boys learning but others who have crushes on you. I'm trying to write your story that can touch each of them in a special way. I want them to see the man behind the bull rider extraordinaire."

"You do take this seriously and overuse extraordinaire on me when I don't even compare to some of the greatest out there," he said, meant it but also at the same time was wondering how she was thinking of him.

"My point is all of them are interested in you. You, not just because you're a bull rider but also they know that you'll be moving forward like all bull riders have to do. They want to know what's next for this thirty-four-year-old handsome cowboy."

"How do you know my age?"

Pearl laughed. "I am a reporter and do my research. Most bull riders retire by this time."

"Right." He should have known that. What else did she know? "Yeah. I'm late and lucky that I had as few injuries as I've had. My parents died in their early thirties, both were thirty-four when I lost them. I was six."

Pearl's expression softened. "You've decided to quit at the same age that you lost your parents."

"That's where I'm at. I hear them telling me to live a new life."

Pearl's hand came across the table and covered his forearm and squeezed gently. "I'm so sorry. I get it now."

He saw the sympathy in her eyes and wanted to get rid of it. "Don't feel sorry for me. I'm tough. I'm strong and I've lived a life that many would want. Bull riders are a set of cowboys all their own. We don't want pity. If you put that in your article then we're done." He meant it. He had felt an unnerving attraction to this lady but now, realizing he'd opened up to her and she felt sorry for him was not what he wanted.

"No, sorry, I didn't mean that." She pulled her hand back and was studying him with a frank expression. "I know you're tough. Everyone knows you're tough. Nothing about this interview is to bring sympathy to you."

They stared at each other. He had softened up because of this attraction and he knew it. "I started my career in anger and there is still anger there. But, also, I realize I loved the challenge that it gave me."

She smiled and her expression was knowing. "That's the cowboy I'm interviewing. I love a challenge too. Believe me you are a challenge."

They stared at each other then he smiled, couldn't help it. "Good. I wouldn't want you to think of me any other way."

And it was true. Yes, he was attracted to Pearl but if there was anything he didn't want it was her sympathy. If… and he meant if, there was something more between them than just this interview then it could not start from sympathy.

He was a strong man and proud of it. He'd walk away from sympathy and this interview in an instant.

* * *

Pearl had almost messed up and she'd realized it the moment the words came out and she saw a fierce flash of fire in his eyes. "In this interview your fans, who love the toughness in you are going to see the way you break horses gently, which I love and so will your fans. They love this masculine bull rider that you are, I'm simply going to show them the strength in you, the masculine horse whisperer who chose to walk away." The tough man with a soft-spoken, gentle way about him, she thought but didn't tell him that was the man before her.

"This is a big magazine. People are going to know you, even people who aren't in the horse industry. Just glancing through it because it's sitting on the shelf in their doctor's office. You know?"

"If it can help someone that's good."

"Brant, you're going to inspire in many ways other than being a horseman, a bull rider. You're going to inspire them just with your life and the choices you've made. This interview and my photos will tell the tale. Trust me."

A gentle breeze was coming across the water now, the sun was starting to set. Pearl's gaze took in the man sitting in front of her and words froze as his gaze held hers.

"You, Pearl McConnell, are the amazing one. I mean, no wonder you are who you are. So well sought out. I don't really care to have my picture taken, but I've had my picture taken a million times. Honestly, this is the first time I'm actually wanting to see it, to see how you see me."

She wanted to see the setting sun's reflection in his eyes— "Well, as I've said, and I'm not bragging, that's what I'm known for," she said, forcing herself back on target. "I'm so glad you came on this trip." She reached out and squeezed his wrist.

Instantly his hand went over hers preventing her from pulling it away. "I'm glad I came too."

Their gazes held.

"Can I take your order," the waitress asked, having not been noticed by either of them. "I can come back."

"No, take our order," Brant said first, smiling at the young lady. "We're ready."

Pearl smiled too. But, she wasn't sure if she was ready for the next hour or so, much less for tomorrow. Her heart was thundering and she was glad she was sitting or she might be unsteady on her feet.

CHAPTER THIRTEEN

After a enjoyable dinner they'd come home and Brant had said good night. He'd left Pearl in the large living room where the glistening reflection of the moon on the ocean could be seen through the gigantic windows. He'd wanted more than anything in a long time to sit out there on that awesome evening, beside Pearl, listening to the waves roll in. Instead he went to his room, the safe place, and now sat on his patio alone… thinking about her.

Varying heights of palm trees hid his patio from the large one downstairs outside the living room and from the small patio across the house from him. Pearl's room.

He looked in that direction a couple of times wondering if she was sitting out there enjoying the same spectacular moonlight glittering on the dark waters of the bay that he was taking in.

He was glad he'd come. Pearl was one smart lady. And there was no denying he was very attracted to her, extremely attracted. Attracted more to her than he had ever been to anyone before.

There was even more to it than that. She had seen what he needed. He hadn't even realized until now, sitting here in the calmness as the ocean washed in and played against the rocks like it was soft music. It was the most relaxing moment he'd ever experienced.

Calmness surrounded him and he began thinking deeply about what his next move was going to be. He was so thankful he'd come. He realized when they were talking at dinner, and he'd corrected her thinking that he needed sympathy. He didn't need or want sympathy. He hadn't continued his phenomenal career on the back of a bull to take care of the anger issues.

He would never have made it to become a champion if anger was his only reason to ride. Yes, getting on a bull's back had been his first driving force and helped him deal with the anger as a young, lost in turmoil kid. But then, once on the back and being good at it, everything had shifted to be about winning.

The challenge. If somebody else could do it, he was going to do it too. If he got bucked off of that bull, he was getting back on, injured or not. He was very blessed, he didn't want to use the word lucky because he knew he worked diligently, training for the moments in the real arena. He rode at least eight bulls a day. Sometimes more and most times in the mornings afterward, he could hardly walk, he was so sore. But he still got up and did it again. And on the side he used his ability to make wild horses into calm working horses to help him make money.

He did everything he needed to prepare himself mentally and physically to climb on the back of the tough bulls he got to ride. Yes, got to ride.

Those bulls were bred from bulls that enjoyed the challenge they'd been gifted with, bucking. Bulls' instincts drove them and the best made the cut and did it for years. He'd ridden and competed on the backs of the best bucking bulls in the country, and he did not take them for granted.

Nor did he take for granted that he had a gift of being able to tame wild horses with gentle words. Whispers and guidance.

Breaking wild horses with calming words and a gentle touch was something he'd been made for but he had also been pointed in the right direction by the best Horse Whisperer he'd ever known.

One night, early in his career, Brant had been

hurting after a rough night and he was eating alone at a diner that stayed open all night.

He'd been sitting there drinking coffee and hurting alone and then an older cowboy walked into the diner. He was an older man who walked straight, no limping like Brant was doing that night from a hurting hip. The man had a smile on his face and asked Brant if he could sit down and have a cup of coffee with him. Brant had said, "Sure" and then he'd recognized the famous Kevin Spark, the Horse Whisperer Extraordinaire as he'd sat down across the booth from him.

He was the best there was and it shocked Brant when he realized Kevin had been watching him and followed him to that diner.

"You're hurting," he said, not a question.

"Yes," Brant had said.

"You feel the challenge and you need it to survive."

It was true and Brant had agreed with him.

Then Kevin had said frankly, "You have a history of anger that needed healing and getting on the back of a bull helped."

"It helps." His anger always eased through his riding.

"That's why I work with wild horses, using my calm voice to take the wildest horses, the most angry horses they have and I can take my calm voice, my calm way of helping them learn to control their anger. I've been watching you and know that you have that ability also."

"What?" he'd asked, startled.

"I've actually watched your career, seen you ride and as you leave you stop by the broncs and spend time whispering to the troubled ones."

He did do that and was shocked that he'd never seen this man watching him.

"I saw you leave tonight, and knew you're hurting bad so I followed you. If you test using your ability of talking calmly to a wild horse, gently helping it control its feelings and emotions and learn to take commands, it can learn to enjoy its life rounding up cattle. Or becoming a competitive ride. Or helping ranchers out on the ranch. I think you would be good at that.

"You put your hand in there, and that horse lets you touch him. It didn't rear up. I've seen many people do that and it drew back."

"You stand back and you watch for that?"'

"I do. I travel a lot to all the big competitions, I enjoy watching them compete. Afterwards, I watch them, the horses. The one you comforted today, that you touched, he's about to be retired and he's coming to my place. I'll work with him to give him a new purpose in life and I'll enjoy doing that for him. It is also calming for me and for the horse. I have a God given talent to help horses but also people when I see their need. And I believe you can do what I do, help horses and people. Not just ride a bucking bull like the champion that you are."

Those words still stuck with Brant all these years later because that night had been Brant's awakening. He'd learned he really wanted to do what Kevin did. So, when he had time off, he went to one of his friends' houses, stayed in the bunkhouse then worked with a wild horse. He'd studied Kevin on videos, watching him use his soft-spoken words and gentle actions to show the horse what he expected. Brant had bought all the same training tools and he'd begun taming horses as he traveled the country and bunked at nearby competitors' places and broke an angry horse.

He and Kevin became friends through the years as he continued to ride his rough bulls. When he had trained that wild horse, it didn't take long and he'd loved calming the horse and helping it become comfortable carrying a rider on its back. But most of all, Brant loved doing the change without whipping the horse, or using spurs or yanking on it too much. He enjoyed making a difference with his soft words, touching its hip with the rod that had the little flag on it. This rod with the flag on it taught the horse to take movement and not go crazy about it. And that's what he had planned on doing for the rest of his life, talking to horses, not riding bulls. And until last night at dinner with Pearl, he had been satisfied.

Sitting there now, looking at the peace surrounding him with the gentle glow of the giant moon, he wondered if maybe one day he might take a chance on loving someone. That also meant taking a chance on losing them like he'd lost his family.

But tonight for the first time ever he knew he might step forward and take a chance on love. Beautiful, calm, amazing Pearl, who had known that looking at the calm of this ocean, the vastness of it. The calmness of it, the draw of it all together might work to open his eyes to more.

At this point, yeah, it was for an interview. He honestly had no idea what he was going to go back to. Did he want to always be the one trying to calm angry animals, or did he want to find a completely different and new life? He rose and headed inside, giving the trees one last glance before he finally climbed into bed and slept with thoughts of Pearl on his mind.

* * *

Pearl was cooking sausage, eggs, and a few biscuits

when Brant walked out of his room. Her heart raced at the sight of him in almost knee length tan swim trunks that showed off muscled legs, slightly white since they probably never saw sunlight, but strong. She imagined that a bull rider's legs were a very important part of staying on the back of a fierce bull. She wasn't sure, but she was sure that Brant was a strong man.

She smiled at him, loving the new look. She hadn't gone to sleep quickly the night before, her brain had been on the cowboy and the article she was ready to write.

Dinner had been eye-opening and she had gone to her room the moment they got back to the house because more than ever, she wanted so badly to sit out on the porch with him.

To watch the moonlight, and feel like she had that day he'd cupped her hand while they watched the moon. She was interviewing him, not dating him. So she had sat out on the private deck overlooking the bay. And like her dad planned years ago, altering the sizes of the palm trees so that where she sat did not have a view of where he sat.

"Breakfast is ready," she said, as she carried the sausage pan over to the table. She placed it on a pad beside the bowl of scrambled eggs while he walked over to the coffee pot and poured himself some coffee.

He held the pot up. "Do you need some more coffee?"

"I'm good, but thanks for asking." He put it back in the machine then walked over and sat down at the table. "I didn't know you were going to cook. I thought you were going to maybe have cinnamon rolls or donuts."

She laughed. "Nope. Sorry. This is what we do. My dad usually cooked it back when I was young, giving my mom the mornings off. So I thought you needed the experience before your first day of fishing in the ocean."

"Thanks. I'll have to make it up to you by catching a lot of fish."

She laughed. "Bingo, that's exactly what you need to do. We're going to have an outstanding day out on the water. I've packed our lunch and afternoon snacks. We'll be back in time for dinner with fish tonight."

"I have to say, dinner last night was amazing, and our talk was too," he said.

He watched her as he spoke and Pearl's insides danced. "I'm really glad. I enjoyed talking to you too." It was true. Oh, how much she enjoyed it. "Honestly, I just have to tell you—well, maybe I shouldn't tell you. But, I travel the world and I don't often—well, I never talk to people like we talked last night."

He nodded then took a bite of his sausage biscuit. His eyes glowed. "This is great, and thanks for telling me that. I don't talk that deeply with anyone."

She knew what he'd done, had to think about what to say, to say the right thing. And he had. Now she needed to do the same, get them back on target for the day, not thinking about how much she'd wanted to kiss him last night. "You're welcome. It's going to be a perfect day because I'm going to watch the bull riding, horse whisperer extraordinaire work his magic on the water and then write about it."

Brant laughed. "I hope I give you what you need out there."

She grinned, filled with such excitement about the day with this man. "You will. Believe me, it's going to be an amazing day."

And she knew it was, because any day on the water, even if a storm was blowing in, was a great day. Being out there with this handsome cowboy was going to be remarkable.

CHAPTER FOURTEEN

"There's Mike," Pearl said after they'd finished breakfast.

Brant looked out the window as the boat pulled up to the pier. "I'll carry these bags for you." He picked up the bags Pearl had sitting on the counter full of snacks and lunch.

"Thanks," she said then led the way out the door and to the boat.

A tall man who looked to be in his sixties stood in the boat finishing off tying it to the pier. He wore a long-sleeved ocean blue fishing shirt with a large swordfish on the front and black long shorts. He smiled and held his hands out to take the bags onto the boat. "Good morning, hope you're ready to fish. I'm Mike."

"I'm Brant, and I sure hope you're ready for a beginner fisherman."

"It's okay. I was a beginner once too. I have to say, when this pretty lady's dad brought me fishing for the first time, I had no idea I would become addicted to fishing. But I did, and am still here taking others out to fall in love too."

"So, Pearl's dad brought you fishing the first time?"

"Yep. We have that in common: We have a McConnell introducing us to the ocean life."

Pearl smiled. "Yes, my dad got Mike hooked on fishing. Got him hooked so much that Mike retired early and became a guide in between fishing for himself. He has a talent for it, an eye for fish similar to yours. He's excellent at what he does like you are at what you do. Therefore, he's the first one I asked to take us out today."

Mike opened a door in the floor to a compartment filled with ice and he set the bags inside. "Let's just say I was persistent in watching and learning. No one can believe that I used to live on a ranch, ride horses, raise cattle, and enjoy my Texas ranch. I loved it but then my friend introduced me to fishing and that's all it took to change my thoughts on what I wanted out of life. Sold my place, moved here and can fish anytime I want."

Brant was a little stunned by that. "You sold your

ranch to become a fisherman?"

Mike grinned. "It was a big ranch and made me a lot of money, so I don't have to make a living at fishing. Nor do I have to run a ranch—which I loved doing at one time. I made a choice to do what I loved, and that's what I'm taking you out to do today. Grab hold of that bar around the awning to give you a little balance as you step onto the boat edge then down into the boat. Once you get the hang of it you won't need to do that but I'm just telling you to grab hold because I'm not going to hold your hand and help you. After all, you ride bulls." His grin grew. "I figure if you have the balance and the stamina to stay on the back of a bull, you can grab that handle, take the rocking of the boat and step onto it all on your own."

Both Mike and Pearl smiled and he laughed. "I just have to say before I take this challenge that if this bull rider gets bucked off this boat, don't tell anybody. I'll never live it down." They all laughed as he grabbed the rim of the awning over the dashboard and stepped onto the boat. It rocked and he rocked with it like he would while sensing the next twist of a bucking bull. Then he stepped down to the boat deck to stand beside Mike in the boat. "That was an easy ride."

"You did great." Pearl laughed then did the same thing he did but without holding onto anything as she gracefully dropped to stand beside him in the boat.

"I can honestly say that looked easy when you did it, and barely rocked the boat," he said, looking at the small, agile beauty smiling at him.

"Ready to catch some fish?" she asked, and he nodded. Ready to spend the day with her was what he was ready for.

"That's the plan," Mike said, watching him, probably seeing that he was attracted to Pearl. "I have a feeling that you're not a quitter," he added, "And you like adventure and challenge."

Yes, he'd seen it alright but was okay with it since he didn't press him on it. "I'm not a quitter. I do like a challenge."

"Good. Never give up on what you want." Mike hitched a brow then continued. "So that's the plan. We're heading out toward the Hump, that's between here and Cuba and down deep in the water. Fish love it and there will be a lot of boats out there. So, when we see fish we'll fish and may not make it to the Hump. Our goal is to catch enough so you can take this pretty gal out to dinner, and enjoy eating the fish that you caught."

"That sounds like a great plan to me. Tell me what I need to do," Brant said.

"Go to the front of the boat and untie the rope. Pearl will do the back as I drive. Once it's untied, push the pole and that'll get us out in the water and I'll take over after that." He turned the key and started the engine.

Brant went to the front of the boat, undid the rope, and then he looked toward a smiling Pearl as she pulled her rope into the boat and dropped it right at her feet. He did the same then, they both leaned forward and gave the boat a shove sending it away from the wooden pier.

Mike slowly drove the boat out into the middle of the lane, and they rode out into the water that he had watched last night. Brant stood there, feeling the water under his feet, liking the rhythm and was able to stand without holding on to anything. He smiled. "This is a whole lot easier than riding a bull."

Pearl and Mike both laughed, gave each other a high five. "We're glad you can do it," Mike said. "It's about to get a little rougher so move to the side and grab this pole on the rod holder because I'm about to hit the gas."

Pearl walked from where she had been standing beside Mike, grabbed hold of the bar that went from the back of the seat to the awning. He was on the other side. "Stand right there so we're on either side of Mike, balancing out the weight. I'm over here on Mike's side because I weigh less than you."

He did as he was told, held on with one hand and watched the houses go by as Mike increased the speed and they were flying into the wind and out to open water. It was a strong feeling of freedom that came with the wind. And he liked it.

Automatically, Brant's hand tightened on the bar, and his legs absorbed the pressure of the stronger waves they hit one after the other. All he could say was this was not a bull and he could easily enjoy the ride, the wind in his face, the amazing blue water and waves they sped through.

They traveled fifteen miles out when Brant noticed some birds flying ahead of them. He hadn't seen birds until now and instantly Mike pulled the bar down that slowed the boat, as he studied the monitor on the dashboard.

"They're here," Mike said, then explained what he was seeing down below. "You saw what first told me there were fish underneath us. It's the birds. Birds know where the fish are. Let's catch some fish."

Mike grabbed a pole and Pearl did too. Mike tossed the line out and handed it to Brant. "This is yours. I'll set up a couple more at the back of the boat. You'll be watching the line to see if a mahi hits one of the lines. If so, put this rod in that hole and take the one the fish is on."

"Will do," he said stepping to the side of the boat and leaning his leg against the side. His back was aching a touch from all the bouncing but not bad. For that he was grateful and knew the time away from bucking bulls was paying off.

"Yes, here we go," Pearl exclaimed, smiling at him as she worked her rod. "If there's one there's more."

He grinned, excited to see her start reeling the fish in so he placed his rod in the holder and moved to her side. "Now, I get to watch the lady work," he said.

She held the rod out to him. "Nope, you're catching the fish today. I'm helping, Mike is driving and keeping us in the fish area, and you my friend are reeling them in."

He gave in with that smile digging deep and took the rod from her, their fingers brushing as they transferred the rod. She'd already explained to him that when the fish pulled too aggressively against the line to give it slack and that was actually the fun part. "Remember, it's give and take, and enjoy the ride."

She was right, he went with the flow of the fish in the waves, and enjoyed the fight. He smiled at her, she was smiling too. "I like it, it's nowhere near as rough as a bull."

She laughed and Mike did too. "You bring it in and when you want I can take you to catch some big tarpon that will make you think when the fight is done that you were on the back of a bull."

Brant nodded at the man. "I may take you up on that." But then the fish pulled hard and swam the opposite direction and the fight was on. He heard the snapping of a camera and looked over to see Pearl had strapped on her camera and was working, and so he did what they were expecting and he reeled in his first mahi to the boat. Mike reached into the water and pulled the beautiful, large fish into the boat. The still fighting fish, which made Brant feel a little bad. But then he knew fish were created for food and so he let that settle in and the guilt left as Mike held the now caught fish out to him.

"Do what he says, hold it like the master fisherman teaches you then I'm taking your first catch."

He did like he was told, took it from Mike, who showed him how to hold it as he stood with his back to the water. Why look at the water when now in front of him and his fish was the smiling intent lady behind the camera.

"This is a large fish," Mike said, a few seconds later after the picture was taken. The man took his measuring stick and declared it a great catch, calling out the length. "Now get back to fishing," he declared as he lifted the lid to a different floor storage area and dropped the fish inside.

And Brant went back to fishing. Relief filled him

after the challenge of the first fish was over and now he was back at it. Almost instantly another fish was on his hook. This time to his surprise the large blue and yellow sparkling mahi jumped high from the water, twisted and then dove back into the water. It was beautiful. He looked at Pearl. "I get it now, this is a totally different challenge."

She smiled widely, her eyes sparkling in the sun and he knew in that instant that the mahi didn't even compare to the thrill seeing her looking like that sent through him.

His rod jerked, almost from his hand as he'd forgotten about it looking at Pearl. "Hang on," she called, obviously seeing that he'd lost his train of thought about the fish.

He did as she said, hung on and fought. And had never enjoyed anything as much as the competition of fishing and the feeling he got with Pearl standing beside him.

Within a few minutes, he reeled in the second fish, not as big as the other but what a fighter it was before he pulled it in.

"Great catch," Pearl said.

Mike slapped him on the back. "Yeah. Two in a row and more out there waiting. I think you have the hang of it."

Within moments he was holding this fish and Pearl was snapping pictures. He looked at her. "Give that camera to Mike and come take a picture with me and this beauty."

"Hand it over, Pearl, he's right. You two need a picture together. And it should go in this article you're writing. People need to see what we see standing here in the middle of these blue waters with a smiling, smart lady. You knew bringing this cowboy out here was going to make a fisherman out of him."

She smiled and handed him her camera. "I wasn't positive, but like Dad knew or thought when he brought you out here stressed out and overworked that you needed a new challenge and he'd been right."

Brant now understood what had happened. Mike had needed fishing for some reason and like Pearl knew he'd needed it, her dad had gifted Mike with this way of releasing tension in a new and great way.

"I have to say, Mike, it is a stress reliever."

"Exactly. Now, you two give me a great picture. You hold that fish out toward me with both hands and Pearl stand slightly behind him with your hand on his shoulder and smile. This is going to make everyone who sees it happy."

Pearl did as she was instructed and Brant did too and when her hand went lightly to his shoulder and she brushed slightly against him for the photo, he knew Mike was the smartest man he'd ever met. The smiling cowboy fisherman saw exactly how much attraction was between him and Pearl, and he wasn't letting it get away without a photo reminder for both of them. Not one or two but several before the grinning captain handed the camera back to Pearl.

"Those are some great shots, if I say so myself."

And though he hadn't seen them yet, Brant knew he would cherish them always.

"Thanks," Pearl said, meeting his gaze as she looked down at the pictures then back at him. "They are great, thanks, Mike. Readers will love them. Now, let's get back to catching more on this amazing day."

And so they did exactly that.

CHAPTER FIFTEEN

B y the time they headed back to Marathon to their house, they'd caught their maximum of mahi mahi. Each fish was beautiful, blues and yellows combined, and Brant couldn't wait to taste them. This was far more than they would eat tonight. When they pulled into the dock, Pearl smiled at her cowboy fishing partner. "It was a great day." It was actually an amazing day. Even more when he smiled, sending ripples through her with that amazing smile of his.

"It was." He looked at Mike. "You were great at finding fish."

Mike carefully pulled the boat alongside the dock. "Yes, it was. Now, you two go shower and dress while I clean the fish so you'll make it to the restaurant in time for them to cook it."

Pearl gave him a hug. "Thanks, we'll be down soon. Just give us enough for dinner and you take the rest home with you. You are a great fish hunter." She chuckled as Mike did too. Her dad always called him that and she knew it was true. Where the fish were, Mike would find them. She had a feeling from watching how quickly Brant adapted that he had it in him too. He'd enjoyed the experience and she'd seen a new light in his eyes. This had been the right move.

"Come on, Brant, we have to hurry to get the fish there in time to be cooked."

Smiling, Brant hopped from the boat after tying his end to the pier as she did hers.

Mikegrinned as she gave him a quick hug once he was on the dock beside them. Brant held his hand out, and they shook hard. "Thanks. You might have made a fisherman out of this bull rider."

Mike laughed as Pearl did too.

"I tried," Mikesaid. "I mean, you know, that's what happened to me. I found a new challenge. I had nothing to do with riding the bull, just riding this boat wherever I want to take it and taking people with me. Anytime you decide to come back, just give me a call, and I'll pick you up, both of you."

Brant nodded. "I may take you up on that. Thanks."

Then she and Brant walked up the long pier toward the huge house that sat waiting for them. When they got inside, she smiled at him. "You loved it, didn't you?"

"I did. Believe me, I noticed you didn't say much."

"I took it all in. Let's go take showers and meet back out here. We're going to go have a fabulous dinner that you caught. It's going to be a great evening."

Twenty minutes later, she walked back out. Her hair washed, semi-dry, casual pants, a soft, tan shirt, and brown leather flip flops. This was their last night, and her head, her brain was whirling with what she was going to write about this cowboy. This man who had skills more than riding a dangerous bull or taming a wild horse. He was a man she saw experience something new today and if she was right it had rocked his world.

Just like seeing him smile rocked hers.

After today, she had figured the man could probably do anything. Her brain was whirling and she was looking forward to their meal. Looking forward to writing an article about this man that she knew everyone would enjoy finding out about because she'd loved being a part of today.

Would love to be a part of his life every day... she'd tried again to push the thought away, the thought that even a cold shower hadn't washed away.

She needed to focus on her job, and as she waited

for Brant, she went to the big windows overlooking the bay. And there he was walking back from the boat with fresh fish in a bag and ready to take them to the restaurant. Her crazy brain instantly went off course again into the deep waters of thinking about him being a part of her everyday life.

She had never thought of a man that way before.

* * *

Brant, fish in hand, found the stunning Pearl waiting for him and they climbed into the Jeep, drove to the restaurant. Music played as they walked side by side to the straw-roofed restaurant by the water, and the loud music playing from inside drew Brant. It was a busy, happy place that instantly expressed the feelings of the crowd enjoying their meals.

Brant let Pearl do all the talking, as she requested an outdoor seat, which got them seated immediately. She led them out to the patio on the side that overlooked the lagoon, a perfect spot, a calmer area. No sunset showing, but he didn't care about a sunset or a sunrise. All he cared about was that he was about to sit down with Pearl, see her heart-throbbing smile and eyes that twinkled as they talked about their adventure. A day he had enjoyed far more than he'd ever imagined.

She was quiet and he knew her brain was working. She had been thinking all day while she fished, grinned, laughed, and watched him enjoy the fishing, just like she had believed he would. He had enjoyed being with her more than anything.

* * *

Pearl's brain was rolling, thinking about the cowboy fisherman sitting across from her. He'd taken to fishing quickly, and he was good. He'd watched her use the reel, done what Mike told him, and then he repeated it all on his own. And he had caught so many fish. She had loved observing him, taking photos of him. She had many to choose from of him with his fish. She would always cherish that first picture and that amazing smile on his face. The cowboy was a born fisherman. She wondered if he loved it as much as he looked like he had. Thank goodness seeing him walking up the trail with fish in hand had put her brain back on target and she'd started thinking about the article. She had to do it justice, write about this cowboy fisherman finding his new way, enjoying life in a free moment, testing the waters of new things that might not just involve raging bulls and taming horses. This man needed life, joy, and more.

So many things were rolling through her brain, but the most was how much she had enjoyed being with him out there for his first fishing experience. She could only imagine seeing the world with him, exploring the places she'd traveled taking pictures alone.

Just that thought had her heart thundering, her mind working, and a wish reverberating through her.

He could train horses, then in his free time they could travel and do photo ops that she had booked. Their lives could work together.

Their lives could work together.

That thought rang through her as she sat there at that table surrounded by happy people.

"You sure are quiet," Brant said, his hands clasped on the top of the table, his glass of ice water sitting beside his hand. Again, she realized no alcohol. The cowboy didn't drink. She liked that too.

She relaxed. Yes, she liked a little champagne every once in a while but not much. Her thoughts immediately went to the toast she and her sisters had done sitting on the deck of Kat's restaurant in Star Gazer, toasting Olivia and then last time toasting Dora's marriage.

Yep. She liked toasting a lot. And suddenly, she wondered what the next toast would be as her gaze met the amazing man sitting before her.

"You really are lost in those thoughts that I can see

rolling around behind those pretty eyes of yours," Brant said, and she realized she hadn't replied yet.

"Sorry, my brain is full with thoughts about the article."

He reached across the table and placed his fingers on hers instantly sending fireworks through her. "I really enjoyed today. You, Pearl McConnell, have an eye that catches everything."

She smiled at his words. "And a brain always working overtime, like it's doing today. I thoroughly enjoyed today, loved watching you enjoy it." It hit her then, the distraction from what she was supposed to be concentrating on. She pulled her fingers from being intertwined with his fingers—a sensation like nothing she'd ever felt before raced through her and she had to make herself let go. But she knew she needed to not focus on those emotions right now. She had an article to think about. She had to get her brain back on that.

She saw Brant's jaw tense, as she pulled away since their gazes held, and then his fingers reached out and gently took her fingers back again.

"I enjoyed it more than I ever thought I could."

She smiled. "I might have liked it a little too much," she said before she stopped herself, unable to draw her hand away and loving that he had held on.

"I get it." He rubbed his thumb along her palm since

he had turned it over so that he could see her hand lying flat on the table before him.

He studied her open palm, as her heart thundered. Then he lifted his gaze to hers. "I fished today because of you. I saw a side of the world that I had never even thought about before. Who would have thought I would be out there fishing? No one but you, Pearl. You not only have an eye for photos, you have an eye for life."

Her heart tugged hard. She'd heard those words before. "Olivia once told me the same thing."

"Olivia was a very observant, smart woman," Brant said, gently.

"Yes, she was." Tears misted her eyes unexpectedly and she wiped them away with her free hand.

"Please, cry if you need to. Or if you need to talk about Olivia I'm here to listen. She sounds like a wonderful person."

Her spirit calmed. "Olivia was a wise one. So many things she said to all of us, knowing she was going to die, still touch us today. I never know when something she said is going to echo in my heart. But the last thing she would want me to do is to tear up and talk about her when, honestly, and these would be her words, 'Girl. You're sitting across the table from an amazing cowboy. Enjoy yourself.'" She smiled.

"I like that." He grinned.

"She knew, like I know, that you're more than that, you're an amazing man. More than a cowboy, more than a bull rider, even more than a horse whisperer. You, Brant, are a man who does well and passes your skill forward with the horses you touch and the kids that look up to you. You aren't out getting drunk or talking bad. You show young men how to do it right. But, I think, you enjoy new things. You just haven't experienced them before."

His palm now covered hers and they held hands across the table.

Their gazes locked. She never wanted to let go and wondered if he felt anything like what she was feeling. It was an amazing feeling.

"Hello. My name is Cassie, and I'm your server tonight. I see that you have some fresh fish there that you would like us to cook for you?"

She went to pull her hand away, but he held on. "Yes. We do. This amazing lady here took me fishing for the first time today, and she and I together caught those fish. And, well, it'll be the first time I've ever eaten saltwater fish that I caught myself. Mahi. So how do you suggest we cook it?"

Pearl smiled, he was getting the hang of it.

"I'll have them weigh them and let you know how many pounds. As for how to cook them, your choices are: pan-seared, broiled, coconut-fried or just fried, and then there's also blackened. You each get a side of your pick."

She pointed at the menu as she looked at the handsome cowboy. "I'll take a baked potato, please."

"Same here. Well, a sweet potato."

"I think I'll take that too. I'm going to be a copycat tonight. I figure if she knew I'd like fishing, and she asked for a sweet potato, y'all must know how to cook them, so I'll take one too."

"That sounds wonderful. Would you like anything other than water to drink?"

"Lemon, please. And I'll probably take a lot of refills. I drink a lot of water."

Pearl liked it. She liked it a lot. The waitress left with the bag of fish that they brought in, and she sat there still with Brant holding her hand.

"Pearl, I know you're going to write this article, and I'm not even worried about what you're going to write. I know it's going to be a great article. You're going to inspire somebody using me, and I'm grateful to God that I can be something like that. I don't always know what someone's going to write, but I know you've been watching. Your brain is working, and I've read some articles that you've written about other people, and it's always good. You don't put their pain in like an open book, their struggles, you put their achievements."

She smiled, her heart throbbing. "I do. And I'll just be frank, you're holding my hand, and I'm having trouble thinking about anything but that."

An engaging smile came to his face, and he said, "I like that."

She knew why he was a horse whisperer. The man's touch and his soft words were mesmerizing. She couldn't and didn't want to move.

CHAPTER SIXTEEN

M y goal is for us, through your story, to help people who need to move forward. Brant, you were amazing today, you stepped into something new with zest. Mikesaw it. I saw it. Did you love it as much as it looked like you did?"

"I did. I now know that there's a world out there other than just riding a bull or taming and training a horse with this natural instinct I have. One of the real horse whisperers saw that and helped me realize it."

"He did. What happened with that? How did you know, did he come tell you?"

He nodded, still holding her hand. He'd never talked to anybody about this. "I was fairly new to riding and winning. Had had a few really rough rides, but I had succeeded. But after riding I wouldn't go out with the guys afterward, instead I'd go find me a quiet diner that would stay open all night. I would eat and drink water and hurt all by myself. Obviously, my friends knew this, one night after the bull had been rough, I had two really rough rides. And the night before, I had also had rough rides. My lower hip, like it's been hurting now, was basically killing me that night. I was only twenty-three at the time. So, it's been about ten years now since the hip problem started. As I sat there alone this cowboy walked inside and came straight over to me. I instantly recognized him, Kevin Spark. I really couldn't believe he'd come straight to me. He was one of the best-known horse whisperers in the world. And I had a thing about that."

"Really," she said, loving this news.

"Yes, I was infatuated with horse whisperers. I had a thing about looking at the horses and the bulls after they've been ridden at the rodeos. The bucking horses were ferocious in their attempt to buck cowboys off. Not just to buck the rider off, they were pretty wild and their anger reminded me of myself."

"'Mind if I sit down?' he'd asked me." Brant had never talked about this to anyone. He thought about it a lot like the other night sitting there looking out over the ocean. Tonight looking into the stunning sapphire eyes of Pearl he told her about that meeting and how Kevin had been watching him and had come there to talk to him. To put the thought in his mind of one day needing a change and horse whispering was a enthralling path for those who had the skill.

He told her how Kevin had stood at the fence but turned away so he wouldn't see him watching and listening. How he lowered his head and spoke softly to the horse, seeing the anger and the hurt in its eyes. And his words and tone, his whispers had calmed the horse.

"I sat there listening to him. Stunned by the man. Knew who he was and what he did and suddenly I knew what he was about to tell me. He said, 'I just wanted to come tell you, one day, the anger in you is going to calm down. And the challenge of overcoming the anger in a different way is going to take over.'" He paused, holding Pearl's gaze, knowing he'd made the right decision. "Pearl, that time is now. I have never told this to anyone but you. Kevin knew I was a born horse whisperer and came to make sure I knew there was a path for me other than the back of a bull. I never forgot that. He was an older guy and had been doing that for years."

"That is amazing and wonderful."

"True. He made an impact on me way back then. I wasn't ready then but I started watching his training online. I watched the horse whisperer work magic on horses. And that's where I learned how to do what I do. Like he said, not everybody can do this. But all those years ago I started training on the side, testing my skills when I was at someone's ranch recuperating after a bad injury. A month ago I had a bad ride, and I hadn't finished it. That's when I knew my back was getting really bad, and I knew it was time for me to make a choice. And I was at a diner, and he walked in again, sat down across from me, looked at me very compassionately. He said, 'I'm just here to tell you. I see it and you know it's time. Are you going to be one of those old dudes that ride till they can't walk again, or are you going to stop and help horses that need you?'"

* * *

Pearl was floored by the story and by the smile that crossed his face and brought tears to her eyes, and her heart ached. "So, here you are going to help horses that need you." She was so thankful for that man.

"Yes. I had already agreed to the interview before I made the decision to stop. The last time I saw Kevin, he was happy for me. The last thing he told me was that one day, you might, like me, want to get married, have kids, and enjoy them instead of sitting in a chair hurting.

'I now have grown kids and grandbabies, I stopped in time. Hopefully you have too.'"

Pearl was struck hard by those words and now knew her article. It was flooding through her entire being and she knew this, her interviewing him, was no accident.

"Brant," her voice wobbled. "Do you know how many people this article is going to help? That it is going to touch people who didn't have that horse whisperer to put that gentle whispering, brilliant voice in your head."

"My anger as a kid without my parents was rough. I could never imagine why God would take my parents from me. But I came to know the Lord as I was on the back of those bulls. Rodeo preachers have a calling and that was one other thing Kevin gave me, told me to listen to the whispers of God and to try out rodeo church. And I did. Now, I don't ask any questions about why my parents were taken so early. I know now that we just have to accept some things. Move forward. And I have peace now, because I know one day I'll see them again." He smiled gently. "And I know that they're happy for me, especially right now."

* * *

Brant felt at peace as he sat there holding Pearl's soft

hand and talking about his past. Talking about his parents' death while they waited on the fish he'd caught that day to be cooked. And all because this amazing woman had an eye for what he needed.

His heart ached suddenly as he looked at her and heard Kevin's words about family. Looking at Pearl he knew he needed her, loved her.

From the first moment, he'd seen her at the auction across the large tent she'd touched him. Put him on alert. And since that meeting it seemed a lifetime had happened in the short time they'd known each other.

More than anything else in his life, other than losing his parents, these few days had changed him. For the better. Pearl was amazing, phenomenal. And she saw what he needed.

"Pearl," he said after a moment. "Would you ever think about wanting to see me after this interview, spend time with me. Because I really want that. Never in my life did I think I would be saying that in this short time that we've known each other, I don't want to lose you."

Her hand squeezed his, and that heart-touching smile of hers spread across that gorgeous face. "I feel the same way. I would have never thought that I would be saying I would like to spend a lot more time with you. Maybe, between you training horses, we could see the world together."

His heart leapt and his gut tightened, and all he wanted to do was kiss her. He leaned forward, unable to stop himself, took his free hand, cupped her face as she leaned toward him, and he gently placed his lips on hers.

There at the table, at the edge of the diner outside, in front of anybody in the world if they wanted to look, he kissed the amazing Pearl.

If they'd asked him what Pearl got to do with making you act this way, he'd simply say, as her lips touched his, absolutely everything.

Nothing had ever felt this strong—

"Here's your food."

He broke away at the soft-spoken words and smiled at the young lady who was carrying two plates.

She smiled. "We've got a lot of plates coming. We cooked your fish, and here's your baked potatoes. The guys right there are going to lay the different types of fish that you ordered in front of you. Can I get you anything else? If not, I'll leave you two, and then your waitress will be back to take care of anything else."

"Thank you," he said. "We're great."

She smiled, her eyes twinkling. "I thought so." Then she turned and left so the guy could set their four plates of fish on the table. They grinned then walked away too.

Pearl had sat silently. But when he looked at her,

she was smiling. "Oh, what a day," she said.

"Yes, it is," he agreed. "And now we're going to test this food that you had me catch for us." Then he took her hand in his. "Let's bless this food."

The smile that came instantly to her face touched him. "Perfect."

And so, he said a quick prayer thanking God for the food, the fun of the day, and for Pearl and her clear vision of what he'd needed, that sometimes stepping out of comfort zones is a good thing.

And though he didn't say it out loud, he thanked Him for sending Pearl into his life.

* * *

Pearl squeezed Brant's hand as he prayed. So thankful for the day. Her mission in life was to use the talent she'd been blessed with and sitting here beside Brant, she'd been given exactly what she was supposed to capture for his story. She now knew without doubt that God had brought her home for this, telling Brant's story. Not for her relaxation, or starting over or finding her way.

It was to be here to accept the interview so she could tell this touching story of a hurting little boy finding his way through the anger that he felt from losing his parents. Then finding his way through the bull riding career and inspiring the young people who followed his career and wanted to ride like he did.

She smiled at him. "I have to say something before we eat this wonderful fish that you're going to love. I know I was supposed to be here to write this story and take the photos. Hopefully, for more than this amazing story, maybe on our personal level that we're creating too. But, I know without doubt that I was put here to tell the story of that young boy who's grown into an amazing man with a fantastic career.

"Kids and young men and women admire you, want to be you, want to watch you ride. I'm here to help tell your story. I want to touch those people, let them know that when one thing ends, it's not the end. It's a new beginning. A new beginning to start all over creating a new step forward. Now you're going to show all those people out there that there are other things too."

Brant looked serious, and she continued. "Think about other people that are hurt like you, young boys, young girls who wanted to be rodeo queens, you know, bull riders, ropers, and something happened, knocked them out of it. The competition days were gone early. Not like you, where you've had a successful time, but their days were gone so early. You're going to show them that there are other options.

"They just need to look for them. Maybe they've had some old guy come in, sit down, and talk to them, whisper to them. And you were not afraid to go out there and do it. Now you're going to make a new life whispering to horses, and I hope seeing the world. And I get to have the honor of telling this story. Thank you. Now I can't wait to watch you in the arena with the horses."

"Pearl, you are the amazing one. I know you've got this interview to do with me and need to focus on that but just to let you know, I'm seriously wanting this to be about more than an interview. My mind and heart are wanting to spend my life with you. I hope that doesn't horrify you. If it does, you just tell me that you're doing the interview and then you're walking away, and I get it. I totally get it because that's how I felt the day I met you. That's not the way I feel now. Minds can change quickly.

"Hearts can change quickly, and I can feel my parents being very happy right now. I see panic in your eyes. Don't panic, it will be what it will be, and I'm good with it. I just needed to tell you that before we eat this amazing fish. Let you know you've touched my life in very unexpected and welcomed ways."

Pearl had to pause her personal feelings for a moment, get her thoughts together for this article.

Everything else, even her heart had to wait, she couldn't mess this up.

"Thank you for those amazing words," she said. "But I think we have to pause. As an artist, a photographer, a writer, a woman who knows this article is important. I can't let myself go deeper. That kiss and this day have tangled up in wonderful ways, but my priority at this moment is this assignment. I have to get this story right, and then we can go from there."

He squeezed her hand, nodded. "You do what you need to do. I'll be here—well in Star Gazer training horses. Or maybe here." He smiled. "I'm hooked on fishing and on you too. I can't wait to see what you're going to write. I hope it helps someone, because Pearl, you are born to do what you do, touch lives."

Her heart swelled, this man had no idea how much he'd touched her life. It was now time to go home and watch him work with horses. Then she had to make it through to the end of the story without throwing her arms around him and holding on like she'd never held on to anything in her life before.

CHAPTER SEVENTEEN

Dinner was amazing, the day had been wonderful and the conversation while eating the fish he'd caught with the woman he loved was unforgettable.

There was no doubt about it, Brant had fallen for Pearl but she was here on business and it came first. She wanted his story to resonate with readers. She resonated with him and he wanted the story to do great for her benefit as well as anyone out there it could touch.

He liked the thought of that, liked it a lot. It wasn't something he had ever actually thought about before. Yes, he'd signed autographs on hats and pictures. He gave kids inspiration when they came to meet him at meet and greets, and he enjoyed doing it. Was glad he could do it. But never had he thought that he could help people who read an article about him.

An article about overcoming a past and fighting not to fear trying new things until they found what was right for them. He had no idea if that was where Pearl's article would go but in his mind, that's what he was seeing. If it could in some way help someone he was for it. He'd had no one until Kevin had walked into the diner and sat down across from him and offered advice.

Advice that had now led Brant to be here on this wonderful evening with Pearl.

They arrived back to the house on the ocean, their last night before they caught the plane in the morning. Though they'd talked he couldn't not ask. "Pearl, it's our last night here and I want to watch that moonlight over the ocean with you."

She smiled. "That's a great idea for an ending to this amazing trip."

They walked outside, the moon glistened on the water, the ocean was soft and quiet. Boats coming in late with their lights shining crossed the bay as he and Pearl sat down in comfortable cushioned chairs beside each other. He held his hand out between them and she placed hers in his, instantly sending happiness through him.

He would wait on Pearl for forever. He couldn't even imagine ever loving anyone else. He never imagined loving anyone, but now his brain was thinking about a life with Pearl. Thinking of traveling together.

What would that be like? Him, the loner, bull rider, now horse breaker and trainer was thinking about going on adventures and watching Pearl do her thing.

"I know you've seen the world, but you wanted to come back here to the beginning of your career. Why was that?"

She smiled in the dim light. "There's something about when you find your way. And when I came to Marathon, I was just a young teenager and had no idea that getting in that water with my camera would change my life. That taking a picture of something I thought was spectacular would attract attention and show me what I was meant for." Her fingers tightened with his. "That's why I came here with you. I felt like you needed to find out that too and maybe this would work for you as well."

He smiled at her. "I can tell you, you got my mind thinking. Thinking a lot about what I want out of life from here on out." He didn't say he wanted what they had right now, sitting side by side enjoying a simple, amazing evening together.

"I loved it." Her words rang through him and for the next hour they sat there quietly, holding hands. Finally, knowing it was time he stood and gently pulled her up and into his arms.

"I'm heading in and will see you in the morning. Sleep well, Pearl," he whispered and then he kissed her on the forehead, not the lips, not now, she was working.

But he'd wanted to. He headed inside thinking about hopefully a future with Pearl.

* * *

The airplane picked them up at the Marathon private jet airport. They didn't have to travel all the way down to Key West this time, Pearl had just landed there to give Brant the experience of being all the way to the tip of the world. They had stopped at Southernmost Point Buoy at the far corner of the USA, having stopped to take a quick picture—from the middle of the road together instead of standing in line to stand beside it. That done they flew straight from Marathon this time and were home within three hours. No matter how hard Pearl tried she kept reliving the moments sitting on the patio holding his hand, watching the moonlit water roll in, and Brant telling her that he loved her.

Thank God she had reacted correctly telling him that she needed to put it off, that they couldn't make decisions like that until after the article was finished and she did that well. When she actually wanted to throw herself into his arms and tell him that she had never felt what she felt when she was around him. But it was true—did she really feel all that strong emotion, or was it just because she was caught up in this wonderful story that was in her mind about this amazing man and his life and how it would be touching people? She had to make sure for herself and for him that what she was feeling was real. And that meant she had to finish the article, had to get it off her mind and to the publisher, the magazine, and then test the waters.

When they landed, they shared a gentle hug. "Will you be out to the ranch tomorrow?" he asked, stepping away.

"Yes, I'll be there ready to watch you work with your horses. Then I'll head home and work on the article."

"Sounds like a plan. I might even make it onto the horse's back by the evening."

"That would be amazing." There was nothing about what he did that she did not find fascinating and she couldn't wait to watch him work.

When she arrived home she almost immediately got her computer out and went to work on the article. It was like an obsession and her brain would not shut down so she worked and finally after midnight she decided it was time to try and sleep. Yes, the article wasn't as long as a book, but there was a lot to think about and to get on paper, and then work on making it all into a shorter article.

She loved it. Writing the article did nothing to stop the emotions she was feeling for the man. Instead it just highlighted everything about him that had made her know that she came back here for a reason. All she could do was pray that together they got it all figured out.

* * *

"I've got two horses ready to work with today. So you can see the difference in starting and ending." Brant watched the way Pearl's gaze went from one black stud to the other, taking them in. She was working today. He had to remind himself of that. Her brain would be working on the article, not on them. "So you see the one outside there, and I'm going to bring in the one I just started working with before we went to Marathon. Okay?"

"Yes. That sounds great. I like knowing that I can see the beginning and the end."

He turned away at that moment when he got the horse untied from the gate it was tied to, then he opened the gate and led him from his pen into the arena. He liked thinking about the beginning and hoped he knew how his and her relationship would end. Happily-ever-after. Yeah. He heard that so often. Never ever thought about it until now, until Pearl entered his life. Now he wanted it. He wanted it more than anything. He'd stayed up late every night since she'd headed home to work on the article thinking about her. Thinking about their great times, thinking about what he'd learned on the trip. He could truly have it all.

He could help animals. Help anyone who watched his career or read this upcoming article. He hoped it would show something good for them, be a positive for them. He could help them through Pearl's article. And he could learn from it and enjoy life. Truly enjoy life like Kevin had wished for him.

Kevin, who was still living his best life in Nevada. He needed to send Kevin a note, let him know that this article was coming out. And, hopefully, let him know that something really great had come from it. But also let the man know what an inspiration Kevin was and had been to him in a much needed time.

His mind busy he led the horse to the center of the arena.

The horse would stop, pull back on him but Brant would give him slack, then gently lead the way after a few kind words of encouragement. "Come on. You can do this."

Yes, he talked to them like they were a child, but it was his way with them that led the way, as if he anticipated their every thought, and he would help them move onward.

They were young in the taming and learning how to live life without struggle. He'd give them a signal with the stick and flag, then soon the horse did as he'd wanted.

Brant understood so well that small things mattered. Taming a horse meant that the horse had to learn not to react the wrong way, not kick, not rear up, get emotional, get angry. If something touched them, when the flag Brant used came down and he nudged the horse in the hip or somewhere else the horse had to learn to react like humans had to learn to react calmly. Life was good when you reacted calmly to things.

Brant was learning that himself and liking it very much. He smiled at Pearl as she was taking notes on words he said to the horse, how he touched the horse with the flag, how he spoke in the ear of the horse sometimes.

He stepped back from the horse. "Speaking in their ear is not something we have to do, but it's calming and that's where the horse whisperer title came from way back in history. But as we know, as humans, ears are important. And for a horse, instinct, hearing and instinct, reaction, it all starts there. When I first brought him out here, there was no whispering going on in his ears. That leg right there was dangerous. If you walk behind him too close, that leg came out, and I had to dodge being kicked. All trainers have their own ways of doing things. So it's not like my way is everybody's way. It's my way. It's what I've learned and what works well for me. I use the flag, and I whisper in his ear. If I'm standing here on the left side, I can take this rod, and I can lift it over his back and wave that flag over near his eye or his ear or in front of him out there. Anything to help him react correctly, not overreact. When I'm on the other side, I do the same thing, and he's learning. Sometimes they learn quickly. Sometimes they're slow. I have a feeling." He reached out with his hand and gently rubbed the horse's neck. It didn't flinch. He leaned forward and spoke in its ear. "I have a feeling you, good boy, are going to be a great horse one day. You have instincts." Its ears flickered. "Calm down." Brant took a side step and then stood straight, then looked over at a smiling Pearl. "He reacted well. I assume you got that."

"Oh, yes. I got it. I took pictures too."

She snapped a few pictures in that instant when he was looking at her. He had been concentrating on the horse and not the snapping of the camera, which wasn't loud. Silence was a great thing. Nothing to startle the horse. He started to turn toward the horse again. "No, stand there, please, beside him like that, and look at me with that expression. That horse whispering man look. Yes, perfect." She snapped several pictures. "Your expression is captivating. And the barn is behind you, and that magnificent white cloudy blue sky, with that amazing strong horse standing there looking at you in the side view, analyzing what you've been teaching him with your simple touch and whispers."

As she spoke, she was snapping. Brant stood there straight like always, his shoulders back, his chin up, his eyes looking straight at her and feeling steadfast emotion that she probably had no idea he was thinking. He wasn't thinking about the horse at that moment. He was thinking about her and the life he wanted to live with Pearl.

She put the camera back down and smiled. "Thank you. I can tell you, readers are going to get so much out of this, not because of me and my writing, but because of you."

"And you," he added, but didn't tell her what he'd been thinking when she took those pictures had nothing to do with the horse but everything to do with her. He loved this beautiful, amazing woman and simply stood still giving her what she wanted so they could move on, get past this interview, and get on with life. Their new life together, he hoped.

With restraint from saying what he didn't need to say in that moment he turned back to the horse. "I'm going to place a saddle on him now. It may take a few tries, but give me time because I told you we would try and step into the saddle." That said, he spent the next hour getting the saddle blanket on his back and then the saddle, and like he'd anticipated from the horse's reactions he took to it calmly.

Pearl watched with complete concentration. "Now, I'll step into the stirrup and then if he handles that, I'll be in the saddle, if not, that will come on another day. Rushing is never a good idea." He also knew rushing love wasn't a good idea either. And was determined not to.

He slid his boot into the stirrup, his hand holding the reins in one hand, calmly against the horse's neck. His free hand on the saddle horn as he whispered calming instructions to the horse. "Be calm, react in a calm way as I stand." The horse had no idea what he was saying but was standing calmly as he lifted his weight from the ground and onto the booted leg that was in the stirrup and in the quick moment he was standing in his left boot his right leg lay against the horse's belly waiting for the moment Brant felt was his moment to lift it calmly over the horse's back and into the stirrup on its other side. As he was thinking the thoughts, Brant did it and in that moment he was sitting in the saddle.

He looked at a startled beauty as she stared at him, camera forgotten as she had only eyes on him.

He wanted that for always. He wanted those amazing eyes of Pearl on him, shining with what he prayed was love.

CHAPTER EIGHTEEN

Four days after going out and watching Brant work with the horses, Pearl finished the article. She sat there on her porch overlooking the ocean, thinking about that last night sitting beside Brant watching the moon and the waves at Marathon in the Keys.

What a wonderful time, a life-changing time it had been. Her thoughts went to her sisters. Dora was so happy sharing her love and travels with her husband Hawk. Like her brother Matt and Kelley, they were so happy. They had someone to share their time with.

Now, here she sat alone after finishing work and knowing it was time to either talk to Brant or get back to her scheduled work taking pictures in incredible picturesque places she would see alone.

Her thoughts went to Hawaii, Kona where Kat was right now. Where Kat seemed to be more often these days than anywhere. Kat the one who she knew would never marry. Her independence was her strong point and after losing Olivia Kat would never risk falling in love and losing the person she gave her heart to.

Pearl had tried hard to think that way and at first it had been easy. Then, she'd met Brant, leaning against that fence after meeting his gaze across that huge tent full of ranchers. One meeting of their gazes and then talking in the moonlight had set the stage for a change of heart. The assignment and the time in Marathon and seeing the man enjoy what she enjoyed sealed the deal.

She loved Brant and after finishing this story about him, the rodeo cowboy who'd made a life of success that his parents would want for him, was now thinking about her sister. She felt a huge dilemma in her thoughts about Brant. She loved him. Loved him so much. And yet, could she take that step forward, commit to loving someone and maybe losing them? With her work she was in control. Of everything, who she worked for, where she worked and the quality of her work. With love… she was not in control. She learned that with her sweet, loving friend.

But she knew when she loved someone, like she knew she loved Brant, that her love for him would continue to grow. And where love grew it would hurt that much more when lost.

With love, she did not have control. Stepping away before she couldn't, she did control.

Kat would never let control be out of her hands. Her strong sister, who traveled like she did, not as many places, but in a similar way. She used her travel to her restaurants as an escape from everything that could hurt her heart. Kat never planned on marrying, never planned on risking her heart. She and Kat were named after their great-great-great-grandmother, Katie Pearl Rayburn. Katie Pearl had lost her mother early, then her father in a tornado that crumbled their cabin on top of her. She'd been trapped alone in the dark beneath and came out unable to enter buildings after that. Her mind had also been mixed up while bad cowboys tried to get her attention so they could marry her and take her land. Katie Pearl was a legend in their family, who was sent a cowboy who was not looking for love but ended up being the one to help Katie Pearl.

The ranch where her brother had gone after losing sweet Olivia had been the old homestead beside Katie Pearl Rayburn, the last name being added after she married the man she fell in love with. But that ranch had been sold sometime in the history and was bought by Kelley because she too suffered from not being able to enter buildings. And Matt had been there escaping his pain and ended up being the one who helped Kelley find her strength again.

Now, Pearl sat here thinking about their family history. It was a wild history of ups and downs and of overcoming. She'd been born to a father who followed in the family history of overachieving. He'd married her mother and they'd started their ranch here near Star Gazer Island because her mother loved the water and wanted to be near it. Her father loved her and wanted to make her happy so here she sat watching the gentle waves in the moonlight near the ranch they'd relocated to.

Sat here thinking about their history that had actually been built of loss and love. On new beginnings. Did she want a new beginning? Never until now had she felt love until Brant. The outstanding man she had just written about, whose article was going to touch lives like it had touched her life. She had lost Olivia as an adult. He had lost his parents as a kid, but like she'd known she couldn't save Olivia; that poor little boy had known he couldn't save his mom and dad. That then took him to the back of bucking bulls. His need to let the anger of that out drove him but also led him to using his gentle whisper to help horses in need. And that would hopefully come out in her article and help people in need. His achievements were astonishing.

He'd let the bull take it out on him, but he had succeeded and not let the vicious bulls take him down. He was now a thirty-four-year-old retiring bull riding legend and her article pointed that out. But gave great credit to the other legend who had seen in him the pain, the anger, and the need. She owed a lot to Kevin, that horse whisperer who had decided to follow him to that diner and tell him that he knew he was a horse whisperer.

And that he'd also had problems in his history where he'd taken his anger out on the back of a bull. But found peace helping horses with whispers of encouragement and training. She was so thankful that Kevin spoke early when he'd first seen that Brant might be hooked on the pain, on the struggle of riding the bull, on the recognition. She was thankful that, yes, he did signings that he would go and meet with kids and inspired them. But behind the scenes, he still struggled with the pain of his past. His loss of the parents his young brain thought he'd failed by not being able to save them.

She was thankful that before Kevin, the man had recognized that Brant had a way with wild horses. It wasn't just his way with softly speaking, which she knew he spoke to her sometimes. That voice, that tone, she loved it. Yes. She loved it. Horse whisperer that he was. He was also a human whisperer. That first night they met, standing there, he was in pain. He was better now, she could tell. Getting off the back of those bulls had already improved him, calmly working with the horses.

She had taken him on that boat because she needed to see if he needed a change. But until they came back, and she saw him truly working with those horses, she had no idea the depth and heart her cowboy had. Yes, her cowboy.

She loved this man, and he acted like he had loved her, but he had not contacted her once since she'd been gone. Since she'd left him there in the arena. She thought maybe he might check up on her. Maybe ask her out on a date, but there had been no contact. And tomorrow would be five days that seemed like a lifetime.

It made her think about the thing that had been bothering her. If she gave her heart to this man, and then she lost him like her brother had lost Olivia, and Kelley had lost her father. And her ancestor Katie had lost her father, could she stand opening her heart more to him and then losing him?

She wasn't sure. Feeling lost, she stood up, picked up her phone, and called their private jet. It was time to talk to Kat. Kat could help her. As she hung up the phone and headed to her room to pack she suddenly felt Brant's gentle touch that night when he sat beside her watching the ocean. He touched her fingers, her hands, her cheek, and he'd spoken to her quietly, asked her to talk about Olivia knowing she needed to get things out.

She wasn't a horse, but she'd loved his touch and his soft words. Maybe there were times when she needed to buck a little bit, get the stored-up anger inside of her out, anger she had suppressed after losing her friend. He'd sensed that.

She stopped packing, her heart thundering. She had a life ahead of her, a happy life.

Her lips spread instantly into a smile. Her heart thundered and the knowledge rushed through her. Flowed over her like ocean water on a calming day. Her smile widened, her heart soared. She loved Brant, whisperer extraordinaire, more than she could deny.

His soft and gentle touch had dug deep into her heart. She knew if he would just choose or maybe if *she* would just choose and open up to him completely, they could have a wonderful life together. They matched. Her career would go with his career. They could relax here in their hometown surrounded by her family and friends, who would become his family and friends.

They could travel the world with her pictures and with his horses that he trained, going to see where they were now and looking to see horses he could help. He was more than a horse whisperer. He was a horse doctor, and she loved him. No denying it.

No wanting to deny it. If he would just realize that loving someone and even knowing that you were going to lose them one day or they were going to lose you, that as long as you had time to love, you had time to live.

Live a truly full life.

That was what Olivia had tried to tell her.

Olivia had lived a short life, but a full one. No regrets.

Pearl strode to the side door, called the pilot and canceled her flight as she walked out into the night. She hopped into her SUV and headed toward the McIntyre Ranch, to Brant. It was confrontation time. It was time to have no regrets.

* * *

Brant had used every power of his being to stay away from Pearl. She had to have some time before he faced her with his heart. No matter what she said, he'd sensed there was still worry about losing the one she might love. And that might be why she'd not come out to see him in the last week.

Time. He alone had all the time in the world. Time

191

to live alone but she'd made her mark, stamped his heart with a love he wanted more than anything he'd ever wanted.

Standing in the moonlight, letting the new horse get used to him, Brant heard a vehicle come to a halt near the cabin. Where the arena was located he hadn't seen the lights come up the long drive. Now, he waited, watching as he saw Pearl come around the porch and stand there in the porch light looking his way.

Heart thundering he dropped the rope and strode across the arena and out the gate. It only took a few long strides to be in the light with her. Unable to help himself he smiled and reached for her.

"I had to let you come to me."

"I get it now. I finished the article and it reached deep inside me like it will reach readers. I wasn't sure why you stayed away all these days, but tonight, sitting on my porch watching the ocean in the moonlight with thoughts rolling through my head, I finally made the call to the private jet and was about to head to Kona to see Kat."

She stepped toward him. Her gaze so soft in the light. "You knew. You Horse Whisperer Extraordinaire knew that I hadn't completely realized I hadn't given up the pain I'd face if I gave my heart to you and then lost you." Tears glistened in her eyes.

"I could see it in your sweet blue eyes. Like I see pain in my horses' eyes. So, I had to give you space."

His heart thundered, he lifted his hand and touched his fingers to her cheek. "I love you, Pearl, like I never knew I could love. You gave that to me by showing me there was more to life than bull riding and taming horses. You awakened me to what I was missing and I found you. You are what has been missing in my life but you have to think the same way."

She smiled, her lips trembled. "I love you, Brant, like I never knew I could love anyone and I want to combine our lives and live life to the fullest with every moment we're blessed with."

He stepped forward and embraced her, heart thundering with hers as he lowered his lips to hers. "Every moment we get is a gift. I love you so much."

"You are my gift," she said, and then her lips met his and he knew that their life was truly going to be an adventure. His heart full, he lifted her feet off the ground as he hugged her to him and she hugged him tighter.

CHAPTER NINETEEN

Kat flew home from Hawaii for Pearl's wedding. When she'd called her with the news that she was marrying Brant, she'd been thrilled at the excitement in her sister's voice. They were wasting no time tying the knot. An ecstatic Pearl had called her and let her know the news, and today was the wedding.

It had floored Kat, but she was happy. Now driving up the drive to her parents' home, where the wedding was being held, she was still processing the fact that both of her sisters would now be married.

It wasn't as if the wedding was six to twelve months away—no, they were getting married today. At least they hadn't flown to Las Vegas like Dora and Hawk had done on a private jet, then surprised them all with the news. But Pearl had said she would have married Brant any way possible—she loved the man so much. But Brant had said he wanted to have a real wedding surrounded by her family and friends, like when they'd met at the auction at the McIntyre's Ranch.

Her thrilled parents had the tent put up on the top hill overlooking the ocean like Pearl wanted, and the view was as splendid and the tent was inviting. Soon, the drive would be filled with cars and trucks as a huge group had been invited. This was a celebration, and the excitement she'd heard in Pearl's voice over the phone line had floored Kat. Made her almost wonder what it would feel like to feel that way.

No. She hadn't wanted to ever risk loving someone and losing them. She had been living her life to its fullest ever since losing Olivia. She loved her life, especially in Kona. For some reason, Kona, Hawaii, was her place of peace. She cooked. She made sure the restaurant was a tourist and local drawing point, and it flourished. But she also fished there. There's nothing like getting on a boat and going out and catching fish herself. Fishing was something she loved to do. Now she was home again where cowboys and ranching were the way of life.

Weddings were too, obviously. And she was actually excited for Pearl. She had arrived late last night, actually early this morning at four a.m. She'd told Pearl she'd be here at their parents' home at four, and here she was about to share being a maid of honor with Dora.

So she was arriving now, driving up the lane to her parents' huge rock beauty of a home. On the way down the road from the main road on their property, she'd passed her brother's spectacular home and was still amazed by it. She loved Star Gazer Island, which would always be her hometown where her family lived. But she loved Kona—it was her place of peace. Her escape—though she no longer called it that, but it had been. Now it was her happy place of peace and tranquility.

The huge white tent came into view there in the huge lawn overlooking the ocean. The tent was huge, so obviously everyone was invited. It was going to be like the ranchers' auction with a wedding and a party and dining here on their hill overlooking the beach and the bay. With the sun setting over the water as they took pictures after the wedding vows were said and her sister was Mrs. Brant Randall. As always, the artist photographer that Pearl was, this was going to make a perfect setting to glow behind photos of the newly married couple.

Kat parked her car, and instantly her mother came hurrying out the side door, her silver hair flying in the ocean breeze. A huge welcoming smile on her face had

Kat jumping from the car, meeting her mom in a bear hug.

"I'm so thrilled to see you and so excited that we get to be involved in Pearl's wedding."

Kat eased up on her hug but kept her arm draped around her mother's waist. "I understand, Mom. I'm so happy that Dora is married and happy, but that was tough on you not getting to hold a wedding for her since they ran off to Las Vegas."

"You know me, I love to throw a party, so she and Pearl are making up for it with this one. Pearl left everything to me, other than where she wanted to stand for the service, but I would have chosen that exact spot on the hillside. It's been quick, but this is going to be the best tent wedding ever. Well, unless you end up letting us give you a tent wedding party with a groom standing beside you."

Kat laughed. "Mom, come on, calm down. Don't get overexcited. This is Pearl's party we're having, not mine."

Her mother's sapphire eyes glowed. "I know, darling. I know. And I get it. But who knows? I'm going to be optimistic. Your father and I have been so happy, and we've been so blessed to have been married all these forty years. Loving someone dearly is worth every moment, even if it's a short moment in time. I told your dad we have to make a trip to Kona to go fishing with you and eat our catch at your restaurant. He needs to visit the ranch there too. We have a new manager, you know. A great cowboy, but we want to come out and make sure everything is running well."

Kat actually hadn't realized the ranch had a new manager. She never visited it—was too busy with her own business.

"Glad he found someone and hope he's good. Now, let's go see Pearl."

"Yes, they are in the pool house waiting for you."

They walked inside the large house. It didn't have glass ceilings like in Matt and Kelley's new home, but it had high ceilings and large glass windows overlooking the bay. This had been her home growing up. But ranching wasn't her love—baking was, and the huge kitchen was where she'd spent most of her time.

"The wedding's going to start here in just about two hours, so that gives you time to spend time together while dressing in the guest house. The dress Pearl picked out for you is so beautiful. The guys are all on the other side of the house, so this is your time with Dora and Pearl. Go have fun."

Kat headed that way, so happy for her sisters and the happiness they'd both found. And her brother too. And her mom and dad. All of her family was happily and almost happily married. But knowing that still didn't change her contentment with her life. She had an awesome life. She walked through the house, down the hall, and out to the pool area. With quick steps she made it to the guest house, which could also be a pool house. Hers and her sisters' favorite place growing up.

She tapped on the glass window of the door, then opened it and stepped inside. "Honeys, I'm home," she sang. Her sisters spun from the mirror.

"You're here," Pearl squealed, and Dora grinned.

Kat stared in awe. "You both look so beautiful. Pearl with her soft ivory hair, and those sea blue eyes sparkling like there is something special happening today—and there is." Pearl wore a white lace wedding dress that had pearls sewn in with the lace, perfect for her sister who was truly a Pearl inside and out. She looked like she'd stepped from a fairy tale.

"And Dora, that soft teal dress is on you." It had one sloped strap over her shoulder, then flowed down around her like it was a waterfall as she swished her hips and made it swirl. "This is my flowing waterfall."

"Both of you look fabulous." Her sisters rushed her and engulfed her in hugs.

"I'm so glad to see you," Pearl gushed, kissing her on a cheek.

Dora kissed her on the other cheek. "I second that."

Kat laughed. "I'm so glad to see you two. Do I have pink lipstick kisses on each of my cheeks for the wedding?"

They laughed, both backing up, each holding one of her hands, grinning as they studied her.

"You do," Pearl said. "But we'll wipe it off when we get your makeup on. Come on. Let's show you your dress. I'm so thrilled to be marrying that handsome cowboy who's going to be waiting for me out on the hillside. Look out the window—isn't it beautiful?"

Kat took in the setting with an arch of soft pink flowers and the blue ocean behind it on the hillside, with rows of chairs lined up.

"It's going to be a party," she said, grinning. "It's beautiful."

Her heart cinched tight looking at this amazing blessing. Her eyes misted as she looked at her sister. "You do know you're making Olivia happy too."

Pearl nodded. Hers and Dora's eyes filled with moisture as they nodded in agreement.

"Now come on and see your dress. We're not in a big rush, but, well, I actually am. I would have sped it up, but my sweet Brant said no. This was our special day, and he wanted to give me everything he possibly could as far as a wedding day and happiness went. Because, he said, I gave him that the night I walked into that tent and met his gaze across the room."

Kat remembered that night just three months ago. It was wild how time flew. "I know that man must be incredible for you to love him like I see that you do."

Pearl nodded. "He is so amazing. We're going to travel together in between the horses he'll be training. You should see the horses he's been taming, calming with his soft words and gentle hands. It's wonderful to watch. Just astounding, actually. And he's my man, the love of my life."

Dora grinned. "I'm so glad for you. There's nothing like finding the love of your life, and now you've got someone to travel with like I do. Like me, Hawk traveled alone, and now I get to join him. You traveled alone, and now Brant will join you."

They looked at Kat. "Don't be thinking about me like that. Y'all know me. I travel alone, and I love it. I absolutely love it."

Her sisters both nodded, gave her another squeeze, and then Pearl pulled back a drape, and behind it hung an beautiful, bright blue ocean water dress. Hers and Dora's were similar, but there was a difference.

Dora was the first to speak. "Our sister gets us. Mine speaks softly. It's the soft teal of the ocean at the water's edge where I search for seashells. Softer, quieter. Your dress is deeper, closer to the horizon on the edge where the water meets the sky. Bright. Brilliant. Vibrant ocean blue just like you."

Kat's heart cinched tight. "I'm stunned by its beauty." And she was. Pearl, standing between her and Dora, wrapped an arm around their waists and squeezed gently. "I have my soft, gentle sister Dora and my all-knowing, strong, vibrant sister Kat. Who has led us all through hard times. When I saw that dress, I just knew that was yours. The same way I saw Dora's and knew that was hers. We are a combination, the three of us put together."

"Yes we are." Kat's heart swelled with love. "This is going to be an awesome day."

"Very," Pearl agreed, as did Dora.

They were so close in hearts and spirits. They had their hard times, but when it came down to it, they were together.

"Okay, sisters. I can't get married without our toast to our lives and sweet Olivia. Come on." She led the way over to a table sitting by the window, and there was set the bottle of champagne and four glasses. One set at the front by the window and already had champagne poured into it. "That is Olivia's glass. I invited Kelley to join us, but sweet Kelley said she loves us dearly, but that this is our time. So, in reality, that glass there is both Olivia's and Kelley's, the two women who've made and make our brother happy. And now this is for us." She poured a little champagne in each of the sparkling crystal glasses as the sunlight hit them. They each picked their glass up and held them toward the center. "This is my toast to us. A sisterhood that's worth everything. Always, even though I'm getting married to the love of my life, this is to us. I love y'all so very much."

"Right back at you both," Kat agreed.

"I love y'all," Dora said, and they clicked their glasses together, each took a sip, and then they set the glasses down and joined together in a group hug.

Pearl pulled her head back and looked at them. "I love y'all so much, and now we have to get you dressed, Kat, and then all of us freshen our makeup. Although you both look beautiful just the way you are. And Kat, that auburn wavy hair is going to look marvelous, so don't do anything with it."

Kat stared at her reflection in the mirror—her dress fit perfectly, and her wild auburn natural curls already looked windblown.

"I'm going to pull it back a little bit. My crazy hair doesn't need to be blowing in the wind, drawing attention from you and your soon-to-be hubby."

Pearl laughed. "It's okay. All my life, that fabulous hair of yours has blown in the wind, and I want it to do that today."

"Well, I'll do what you want." And so she did. This was Pearl's special day, and she was the one with the eye for extraordinary pictures, so she would get Kat's wild hair running free in her wedding photos.

And she knew that in Pearl's eyes, as she was buying these dresses and thinking about her hair and Dora's beautiful hair and her hair and where the wedding was being held, she was thinking about the pictures. It was a natural thing for Pearl, the picture taker. She couldn't wait to see them.

"You're going to be so book for weddings."

Pearl smiled. "We'll see. I have a lot of magazines booked already on all the different things. And being here with Brant in between photo shoots, helping him calm horses is going to be wonderful. We'll be working things in, but also limiting them too."

There was a knock on the door.

When it opened, there stood her mom and her sister-in-law, Kelley. Pearl waved her arm at them. "Come on in and join the party."

They came in smiling. Her mother looked delighted to see the happiness. "It's time, sweet Pearl. Your dad is waiting, and you two look lovely," her mother said. "All my girls look gorgeous." She looked at Kelley. "We're glad to have you in the group."

"I'm so glad to be here. This is going to be a

beautiful wedding. Mom, you go get in line, and my hubby is walking you in. Then he comes back for me. You two walk beside each other. And then you and your dad, who is waiting out there for you. Okay, here we go."

Pearl loved that Kelley had helped get everything organized with her mother. She loved the whole family and each new person who had been added to their family.

The music started, and they watched from the door as Matt crooked his arm out and their mother slipped hers in, and then walked with him to the front seat. Then he came back for Kelley, looking so happy.

Then it was hers and Dora's turn. Their dad gave each of them a hug, and then they walked slowly down the aisle together, then took their spots and watched as Pearl came down the aisle with their father.

Pearl's heart showed in her eyes as they met Brant beside the preacher. His gaze locked on Pearl. *What would that be like?* The thought struck her hard. She wasn't interested. But then the wedding song started.

Pearl and her dad walked down the aisle, and everyone stood up. The breeze blew as they made it to stand before the preacher.

"Who gives this bride away?" the preacher asked her dad.

"I do." And then he traded Pearl's hand that was on his arm into the waiting hand of Brant.

He wore an endearing smile. "I can't wait to make you mine."

"I can't wait either," Pearl said softly. And they turned together to face the preacher.

And there, on that spectacular landscape surrounded by smiling people, the preacher told everyone to have a seat, and the vows began.

Beautiful words came from the pastor, then Pearl's sweet "I do," followed by Brant's deeply serious "I do." Then the now-smiling preacher pronounced them man and wife. "And you may kiss your bride."

Kat felt a tight emotion inside as Brant tenderly took Pearl into his embrace and kissed her. Their hug tightened, and then to everyone's surprise, Brant scooped Pearl up into his arms, one arm beneath her knees and one around her back as he spun around and they kissed.

Pearl's hand cupped his cheek as he said, "This is going to be the best life ever, amazing Pearl."

Pearl pulled back with a huge smile. "Mister Horse Whisperer Extraordinaire, I love you so much. Now let's get this party started."

He turned to face everyone, but instead of them walking down the aisle together as man and wife, Brant carried Pearl in his arms like a trophy with a big grin on his face.

Kat watched it all, her heart thundering, and she couldn't, for that instant, help but feel a longing to have something like that with a man.

She and a smiling Dora walked down the aisle and then into the tent where everyone else followed. Music played and the party did start. And seeing Brant set Pearl on her feet, then hug her as they started dancing, Kat felt an incredible sense of happiness… and longing.

About the Author

Debra Clopton is a USA Today bestselling & International bestselling author who has sold over 3.5 million books. She has published over 81 books under her name and her pen name of Hope Moore.

Under both names she writes clean & wholesome and inspirational, small town romances, especially with cowboys but also loves to sweep readers away with romances set on beautiful beaches surrounded by topaz water and romantic sunsets.

Her books now sell worldwide and are regulars on the Bestseller list in the United States and around the world. Debra is a multiple award-winning author, but of all her awards, it is her reader's praise she values most. If she can make someone smile and forget their worries for a few hours (or days when binge reading one of her series) then she's done her job and her heart is happy. She really loves hearing she kept a reader from doing the dishes or sleeping!

A sixth-generation Texan, Debra lives on a ranch in Texas with her husband surrounded by cattle, deer, very busy squirrels and hole digging wild hogs. She enjoys traveling and spending time with her family.

Visit Debra's website and sign up for her newsletter
for updates at: www.debraclopton.com

Check out her Facebook at:
www.facebook.com/debra.clopton.5

Follow her on Instagram at: debraclopton_author

or contact her at debraclopton@ymail.com